Five reasons wh

# YOUNG HOUDINI

## The Demon Curse

A **mystery** to solve

**Death-defying** stunts and tricks!

Do you know about the famous **magician**,
Harry Houdini? What about the boy?

Fast-paced, **edge-of-your-seat** story

Be prepared to be **amazed!**

# Note from author, Simon Nicholson

Harry Houdini was the most famous magician and escape artist of his time—probably of all time. Throughout his adult life, right up until his death in 1926, he dazzled his audiences by subjecting himself to spectacular ordeals. He escaped from nailed-shut crates thrown to the bottom of rivers; he broke out from one of the most secure cells in the District of Columbia jail; he writhed his way out of straitjackets while dangling from tall buildings. Nothing defeated him—no one could explain his mysterious powers.

He wasn't just a magician, either. As well as being the world's most famous illusionist, he also devoted much of his life to doing battle against 'magic'. Indignant at the thought of ordinary people being exploited, he worked ceaselessly to expose false mediums—con-men who duped their victims into believing they could summon their long-lost relatives from beyond the grave. In his stunts, Harry pulled off amazing escapes; but he also sought to set his audiences free, rescuing them from the manipulative clutches of fake 'miracle-workers'.

So that was the great Houdini. But how did he acquire such phenomenal skills? I couldn't stop thinking about what might have happened to him as a boy to turn him into such an extraordinary man.

A fair bit is known about Houdini's childhood. He emigrated from Budapest, Hungary, to America with his family when he was just four, and grew up relatively peacefully in Appleton, Wisconsin. No records of derring-do or mystery-solving. But much intrigue surrounds Houdini's adult years—some people believe he led a double life as a spy, working for the American and British governments. I started wondering if perhaps Houdini could have had another double life too, one that happened in his childhood? What if the few facts we know of Houdini's early years—Wisconsin, the peaceful childhood—turned out to have been a cover-up, devised later in order to conceal a far more thrilling and dangerous truth?

What if Houdini actually moved to America when he was a slightly older boy—and under mysterious circumstances? What if he became separated from his family on the journey—and fell in with two friends, not to mention a secretive crime-solving organization? After all, the real Houdini did a fair amount of tinkering himself with his life's events. At one point, he claimed to have been born on American soil, not in Hungary at all; and of course he was brilliant at creating intrigue around the secrets behind his extraordinary tricks. He even hired the horror and mystery writer H.P.Lovecraft (a favourite author of mine) to write a made-up tale about him having an adventure in Egypt, in which he investigated sinister forces beneath the pyramids . . .

Maybe, I decided, it was time for even more mystery. Mystery about what might have happened to Harry Houdini—the boy magician.

*To Dominic and Tristan Teverson*

# OXFORD
UNIVERSITY PRESS

Great Clarendon Street, Oxford OX2 6DP
Oxford University Press is a department of the University of Oxford.
It furthers the University's objective of excellence in research, scholarship,
and education by publishing worldwide. Oxford is a registered trade mark of
Oxford University Press in the UK and in certain other countries

Database right Oxford University Press (maker)

First published 2015

British Library Cataloguing in Publication Data
Data available

ISBN: 978-0-19-273476-1

1 3 5 7 9 10 8 6 4 2
Printed and bound by CPI Group (UK) Ltd, Croydon, CR0 4YY

Paper used in the production of this book is a natural,
recyclable product made from wood grown in sustainable forests.
The manufacturing process conforms to the environmental
regulations of the country of origin.

# SIMON NICHOLSON

YOUNG HOUDINI

The
Demon Curse

OXFORD
UNIVERSITY PRESS

# Chapter One

Harry woke up. Or, at least, he thought he did.

Blackness, everywhere. He closed his eyes, and then forced them open, but it made no difference. Only the flutter of muscles in his face told him that he was opening and closing his eyes at all. He tried to move, but his legs, arms, and head were jammed. He fought, but his body stayed trapped, and the effort made him gasp as he tried to suck in air.

*Breathe.* His heart pounded, blood throbbing in his veins. The air around him was hot and stale, and when he drew it in, his body just ached for more. His head spun, and he felt a prickling sensation in his fingers, spreading into his hands. *Desperate for oxygen.* He sucked in another useless breath, but the sensation kept spreading. *Concentrate. Stay calm.*

His left hand swivelled slightly at the end of its wrist. His prickling fingers roamed about, exploring.

He was in some sort of box. Its sides were rigid, holding his body, but his fingertips detected a thin lining. *Silk, perhaps?* Harry's heart beat harder and his breathing sped up, pain jabbing in his lungs like a knife. He gathered his mouth into a tiny hole, and forced himself to breathe through that. *Make the oxygen last.* Angling his hand, he let his fingertips creep along the lining of the box, until they found something hard, square, and metal.

*The inside of a lock.*

Harry forced the remaining air out of his lungs. His body fought, trying to cling on to every wisp of breath, but he pushed it all out so that his shoulders sunk and his ribs caved. In that tiny released space, he managed to swivel a leg upward just slightly, until the boot was braced against the box's inside. He breathed back in, and felt the box tighten around him. But his boot was in position, his leg hinged at the knee. His lungs ached, his head spun from lack of air, but he managed to kick, hard, and the box gave, just a little. Two cracks of light flashed briefly on either side of its lock. Harry's hand angled in a new direction, his fingers pushing through the lining's stitching, searching for what he needed.

He found it, just a couple of inches away. A sturdy metal staple, fastening the lining in place. He wriggled his fingernail beneath it, levered it up, and spun it in his fingers, straightening it. Harry braced his leg again, and kicked even harder. The cracks of light widened, and Harry's leg held the lid like that, muscles shaking. He squeezed two fingers through the gap, the staple gripped between them, as the edges of the crack bit into his flesh.

The edges bit deeper. The muscles of his leg were giving way, and the darkness of the box filled with hissing as his breathing grew even faster. He realized that his fingers and hands were no longer prickling, that a cold numbness was taking hold instead. *Need air* . . . His head spun again, and he saw visions dance in the blackness—a locked suitcase with two fingers prodding out of it, pale and weak, a little straightened-out staple falling away from them onto the ground . . .

A last shudder of strength in his leg. The gap widened, and his fingers wriggled out further. Through the numbness, he could just feel the shape of the staple, gripped between a finger and thumb. It was there, he knew it, and he angled it towards where the keyhole would be.

He thrust the staple in. He felt it bump against the lock's innards. He pushed an ear against the inside of the box, and listened to the noises: a spring stretching, a latch grinding. He could feel nothing at all in his fingers now as he moved them about, but he could hear the sounds, allowing him to go about his work.

*Click.* A latch fell into place. *Click.* Another one. Harry's boot pushed even harder, widening the crack, allowing his hand to reach further, his fingers to re-angle the staple one more time . . .

*Click.*

The box sprang open and the cracks became a blaze of light. Harry toppled out, and fell onto a shuddering wooden floor. Everything was shaking—the cushioned seat next to him, the wood-panelled walls. Harry blinked in the brightness, and looked up at a trembling iron rack on which was a torn-open silk-lined packing case. *A railway carriage compartment.* He took in the sliding door, the fan rotating on the ceiling. Then he saw the window and flung himself at it, pulling up the lacework blind, pushing down the sash, and sucking in deep draughts of air.

A river blurred past, followed by a tangle of palm trees. The air felt warm and moist. His gasps slowed, his head stopped spinning, the feeling crept back into his skin. Harry looked down at his hand and saw, still gripped between his fingers, the straightened-out staple. The corners of his mouth curved slightly upwards. Turning away from the window, he pocketed the staple, and couldn't help putting a foot forward to perform a small bow. *Sheer habit*, he thought.

But then he heard the voices. He snapped upright again.

'Mmmpf . . .'

'Get me out . . .'

For the first time Harry noticed the iron rack on the *other* side of the compartment. He saw what was stacked on it—two more suitcases. He was up on the cushioned seat, his heart pounding again. Struggling noises drifted from the suitcases, along with muffled voices, getting weaker. Harry's hands shook as he fumbled in his pocket for the staple. *Hurry.* Pulling the staple out, he forced it into the first suitcase's lock.

'Hang on!' His voice cracked. 'It's me! I'll get you out—'

'Harry?' a voice cried out. The case on the left jolted. 'Is that you?'

'Quick . . .' The voice from the other case was faint. 'Help me . . .'

The first lock sprang open, Harry threw open the lid, and a girl toppled out. Billie had dark skin and tightly curled hair, and was wearing a scruffy factory smock. Harry managed to grab her as she fell, so that she bounced safely onto the cushioned seat below.

'Artie . . .' She sprawled there, gasping. "You've got to get Artie out too . . .'

Harry went to work on the second lock. A few seconds later a boy in a tweed suit fell out, thudding onto the cushioned seat next to Billie. Harry collapsed down between them and, for the second time, tried to get his breath back.

'What's going on?' the girl spluttered.

'Don't worry about that for now, Billie.' Harry grabbed her arm. 'Are you all right?'

'I think so . . . Good thing you rescued us. Reminds me of the time I was locked in a cupboard by the head chef of that hotel kitchen I worked in, back in Chattanooga—did I ever tell you about that?' Billie managed a smile, and then stared up at the suitcase on the opposite rack. 'How did you get yourself out, anyway? Tricky stuff, even by your standards.'

'I'll tell you later.' Harry turned to his other friend. 'Hang in there, Artie, you'll feel better soon.'

'I know . . . I could breathe in there but only just . . . It'll take a while for my blood to re-oxygenate completely . . .' Arthur loosened his tie, and pulled in another deep breath. 'But where are we? I think it's safe to say we're not in New York anymore.'

He stumbled over to the window. Harry and Billie joined him, gripping the windowsill and taking in the scene. More palm trees swept past under a hot grey sky. The train curved and raced alongside a huge river, with a rippling brown surface that glittered in the sun.

'Definitely not New York,' Billie muttered. 'Palm trees, that's the big clue.'

'I'd say we must be two hundred miles south at least, given the palms and the high temperature.' Arthur's voice had steadied, his English tones neat and precise. 'I can't make head or tail of this. Last thing I properly remember, we were back in the theatre in New York helping Harry with his spectacular escape act and—'

'And then that letter was delivered, and we opened it.' Billie's eyes narrowed. 'That letter we read, all three of us—and a few seconds later we were flat on the floor, all three of us, collapsing in some kind of drugged sleep.' Her eyes narrowed even more, and she pointed. 'That letter, which is still in your pocket, Harry, RIGHT THERE.'

Harry looked down and flinched. There it was, a folded piece of pale green paper, poking out of his jacket pocket. Arthur was already holding out a handkerchief, and Harry used it to gingerly pull the letter out. He too thought back to that moment: the three of them sitting in the theatre office. He remembered the act the three of them had just performed, full of the usual tricks involving razor-sharp knives, handcuffs and fire, and finishing with the most spectacular stunt of all, which involved him escaping from a small iron cage that had been plunged deep into a vat of water. *Thrilling stuff*, Harry thought, with another smile. Then he focused on the letter again.

'There was some sort of dust on the paper, which came away on our fingertips—now I think of it, I remember that too.' Arthur had taken a magnifying glass from his pocket, and was peering through it at the letter. 'Gone now, by the looks of it. Still, it certainly was powerful—knocked us out cold.'

'It's not just the paper we need to think about but what the letter actually says. That's pretty odd too,' muttered Harry, reading it one more time.

*To Harry, Billie and Arthur,*

*You have impressed us greatly. But your greatest achievements lie ahead of you—we will make sure of it.*

*Sent with the consent of The Order of the White Crow*

'The Order of the White Crow . . .' Arthur frowned. 'Anyone got the faintest idea what that might be?'

'Nope—in fact, there's not a single bit of that letter that makes much sense, if you ask me,' Billie said. 'This sure is a mystery . . . Reminds me of the time I woke up and discovered I was tied up in the hold of a shrimp-boat off South Carolina, been press-ganged into another crummy job obviously, but it didn't take me long to escape and—WATCH OUT!'

Billie flung herself back against the compartment wall, and Arthur did the same. Harry took care to hold his breath, and extended his arm, so that he was staring at the letter from as far away as possible. Beneath the handwriting, whitish wisps floated from the page and more words appeared. Harry carried the letter to the window, where the breeze snatched the wisps away, leaving only the words.

*P.S. Congratulations. If you are reading these additional remarks, then you are successfully launched on your mission, and it is safe to reveal more. Regarding the suitcases, we apologize, but secrecy is vital, and so we had to smuggle you out of New York entirely unseen.*

Concealed air holes were drilled, a convenient staple was left near Harry's hand for when the drugs wore off—we expected you to manage the rest. Now, you no doubt wish to be told about our organization and its purpose? Perhaps it is simplest to say this: that it exists to unmask and defeat evil-doing wherever it may lie, and that it seeks to recruit those capable of helping that noble cause. Prepare yourselves for your first investigation . . .

'That's some letter,' Arthur said, peering over Harry's shoulder as the last few wisps drifted away. 'Not only coated with knock-out chemical dust, but it's got some kind of light-activated invisible ink on it too.'

'Sure—but what's it actually saying?' Billie pointed out. 'It says it's revealing more, but it's just making things even more confusing if you ask me.'

'It's right about the staple.' Harry held the piece of metal up in his other hand. 'I'd have found something else to pick the lock anyway, but it was handy bumping into this straightaway.'

'And guess what; here are the air holes. Rather small, but they're there.' Arthur tore back the lining in one of the open suitcases, revealing a row of drilled holes. 'Still, *defeat evil-doing*—what's the meaning of that? As for wanting us to carry out some kind of investigation . . .' He put his head on one side. 'Actually, maybe that bit *does* make sense.'

*It does*, thought Harry. He closed his eyes, and his thoughts travelled back again, not just to their time at the theatre, but to the rather unusual events that had taken place shortly before. The whole of New York had been baffled by it—the mysterious disappearance of an elderly stage magician from his dressing room in an inferno of purple fire and smoke. No one had been able to solve it, but he, Billie, and Arthur had investigated the business and, after various adventures including a break-in at a hotel, a terrifying tightrope walk between two ten-storey buildings, the discovery of an ingenious secret doorway and a showdown with one of Manhattan's most ruthless villains, they had uncovered everything. And all the time, he reminded himself, someone had been watching them, following them . . .

'I saw him,' Harry muttered, opening his eyes.

'Saw who?' Billie asked.

'The man who sent us this letter.'

'What?'

'I remember seeing a man watching us from the street, when the letter was delivered. About fifty years old, wearing a pale suit . . .'

'How do you know it was him who sent it?' Arthur frowned. 'Just because he was nearby when it arrived—doesn't mean anything.'

'I'd seen him before. When we were carrying out our investigation back in New York, he was following us, I'm sure of it.' He closed his eyes and saw him again. *Those piercing grey eyes.*

'Maybe he was just interested?' Billie pointed out.

'It's a bit of a coincidence,' Harry mused.

'BREAKFAST IS SERVED!'

The compartment door rattled open and an attendant wheeled in a trolley, crowded with silver-domed platters. Elderly, plump, and wearing a uniform that had gone a little mouldy in the heat, he positioned the trolley in front of Harry and his friends, and bowed. Harry folded up the letter hastily, and glanced back through the window. The train was still rattling alongside the river, but he could make out some broken-down buildings on its far side and, peering ahead, he saw more buildings still.

'Did everything your friend requested!' The attendant rose from his bow. 'Every particular!'

'Our friend?' Billie asked.

'Why yes, young missie. You must know him? Tall fellow, wearing a pale suit, and with an ever-so-neatly trimmed white beard.' The attendant pointed back into the corridor. 'I met him out there last night. Standing outside the door, he was—the curtain was down and he showed me your tickets and said you weren't to be disturbed until ten minutes before the train arrived. And that's now!' He lifted the dome from a platter, revealing bacon, eggs, and sweet-smelling plumes of steam. 'Tipped handsome too, your friend.'

'Hmmm.' Arthur lifted a silver fork, and gave the bacon a careful prod. 'So, in ten minutes, this train is going to arrive—where exactly?'

'This is the Crescent Express.' The attendant lifted another dome, revealing pastries. 'Only one place it can be heading—the great southern city of New Orleans!'

'New Orleans?' Billie gasped.

Harry saw her reflection, curved out of shape on a silver dome, and then looked at Billie herself, and thought that she was a little altered too. Various expressions were flashing across her face: interest, puzzlement, and even a flicker of sadness, and Harry was about to ask her about it when he saw something else out of the corner of his eye, and swung towards the window.

Another train was hurtling along beside them, on tracks about twelve feet away. Hovering in one of its windows, a face.

'Say . . .' The attendant stared at the other train too. 'Isn't that your friend? Right . . . there?'

*A pale suit. A neatly trimmed beard.*

It was the man Harry remembered from New York.

'Harry!' Billie yelled.

But Harry had already pushed down the handle of the door. He threw it open, the billowing wind slamming it against the carriage's side. Pushing away the breakfast trolley, Harry took two steps back from the open door, four steps, five. He crouched down, and felt his whole body tense as he prepared to run, and leap across to the other train, just twelve feet away.

'Harry, don't do it!'

Arthur's voice shouted in his ear. At the same time, he could feel hands grabbing him, pulling him back, hands that belonged to the orderly, and to Artie and Billie too.

*They've got a point*, Harry thought, as he stared out at the other train.

It was curving away. It wasn't twelve feet away anymore, it was fifteen feet, twenty feet. *Too far*, he thought. *Even for me.* But he kept his gaze fixed on the other train, and at the man staring right back at him.

He was exactly as Harry remembered him. His pale suit was immaculately tailored, his beard neatly trimmed. But it was the stare that Harry recognized most, even though the man was some distance away. *Two piercing grey eyes . . .*

The other train curved off to the west, and the face drew away until it became a dot, a tiny pale smudge.

Harry kept watching.

But then the train hurtled behind some buildings, and the man in the pale suit vanished from view.

# Chapter Two

'Orleans Central', said Harry, reading the large sign welcoming them to the station. He jumped down from the train and swept along the platform, dodging the other passengers as they heaved their luggage out of the carriages. Trolleys rattled, porters shouted, and steam billowed from the train's engine, blotting out the late-afternoon light. Harry took a bite from a pastry, grabbed from the breakfast trolley as he left. Beside him, Billie and Arthur munched on various breakfast snacks too.

'Tasty.' Arthur nibbled at a sausage. 'That's one thing we know for certain about our friend—he puts on a good breakfast.'

'Sure, but it's the *only* thing we know.' Billie wiped bacon grease from her mouth. 'Unless any more magic ink's shown up on that letter, Harry?'

'Sorry, no.' Harry checked the letter again.

'So we're still in the dark,' Billie tutted. 'All we can be sure of is that we're mixed up with someone who's bought us breakfast and works for an organization that's perfectly happy to drug three kids, lock them in suitcases, and transport them hundreds of miles away.'

'It's also an organization that unmasks and defeats evil-doing, remember?' Harry tapped the letter, safe in his jacket pocket.

'So we're told.' Arthur fished out a leather note-book from his pocket, flicked through pages of purple handwriting, and twiddled a fountain pen. 'Look, if you ask me, we should get the next train back to New York. Apart from anything else, Harry, we need to keep working on our act at the theatre.' He jotted a few notes. 'Escaping from the underwater cage is all very well, but we've got to keep thinking up more ideas for death-defyingly dangerous magic—our fans will get bored otherwise. I've been writing down some thoughts . . . have you had any?'

'One or two,' said Harry. They were out through the platform gate, and he had noticed a food stall, standing a short distance away across the ticket hall. Fresh fish sizzled on a grill. Coals burned furiously below.

Harry's thoughts snapped back to the moment in the train carriage, his friends holding him back. They had been right to do so—but the energy of those few seconds still quivered inside him, and it would be a waste not to use it. Besides, his friends had noticed the burning coals too.

Harry stared at Billie and Arthur, and they stared right back, nodding.

Billie hurried across to the stall owner, and talked to him. Arthur ran to another nearby stall and fetched Harry a glass of water. Soon, Billie was fishing amongst the coals beneath the grill with a pair of iron tongs, while Arthur marched up and down, attracting the attention of a few passers-by.

'Prepare to be amazed!' He waved his arms. 'Prepare to be astounded! Prepare to witness Harry Houdini, the boy who has no fear! For what need has he of fear . . . when magical powers are in his grasp!'

*Nicely put*, thought Harry. Arthur was good at speeches, and he had done a good job with making up that name for him too, back in New York. Harry drained the remains of the glass of water, handed it to a man in the crowd that had gathered, and stepped forward. Billie was holding up the tongs and, gripped between them, was a coal, bright red with heat.

She threw it straight at him.

Harry thrust out a fist and jerked it upwards just as the coal hit. As the coal flew up into the air, pain bit into the skin of his knuckles, but he ignored it, keeping his eyes fixed on the flaming coal as it fell back down again. This time he bounced it off his arm, and he saw wisps of smoke curl from the point where it had hit his jacket sleeve. Next, he caught it on his boot, kicking it up in the air again as high as he could. As it started to descend, he turned to the crowd, and raised an eyebrow. Then he held up an arm perfectly straight, and tilted back his hand, so that the opening of his sleeve gaped, waiting.

'Behold Harry!' Arthur cried. 'The boy whom fire cannot harm!'

The coal gathered speed as it rocketed downwards, glowing white. The crowd, Harry noticed, was already quite big, and every face was totally absorbed in the trick. He stared up, and muttered a few phrases of Hungarian, his old language, knowing that the unfamiliar words would sound mysterious, magical even, to his audience. His arm remained upright, and he tilted his hand even further, so that the sleeve was open wide enough.

The blazing coal shot straight down inside it.

Screams from the crowd. A woman fainted, collapsing into her friends. Harry, contorting his face with expressions of pain, clutched at his wrist, then his elbow, then the base of his arm as the coal tumbled down inside his sleeve. He clutched at his chest as it travelled under his shirt, burning into his skin.

*Except it's doing no such thing,* he thought, with the tiniest smile, as he whisked the upright arm down and glimpsed, trapped between the hem of his jacket sleeve and the thick cuff of his shirt, a fiery glow. A flick of the wrist had caught the coal there, and another dart of his arm tipped it into the side pocket of his jacket, as his other arm continued to hold his audience's attention by furiously clutching at his stomach. He tugged at his belt, and started to mime the descent of the coal down the inside of his left trouser leg, gritting his teeth with pretend agony. He glanced down at his jacket pocket, and saw wisps rising from it, but he knew he had a few more seconds, thanks to the fact that he had tipped half of the glass of water down his sleeve just before the trick began.

Another wince of pretend pain. Harry crouched down, and scrabbled at his left ankle, as if the coal was stuck there.

*A flash of an arm. A flick of a wrist.*

The coal was out of his pocket, lodged beneath the heel of his boot. No one saw, too gripped by the way he was scrabbling at his ankle. Harry sprang away, shaking his leg, and there the coal was, lying on the ground just as if it had dropped out of his trouser leg. He gave it a skilful kick, sending it flying up towards Billie, who was waiting with a bucket of water. It shot straight in, and disappeared in a hissing cloud of steam.

The audience burst into applause, clapping, cheering, and waving hats in the air. During the short time of the trick, the crowd had nearly doubled in size, and Harry spread his arms wide and lowered himself into his usual bow, straightening back up in time to catch every one of the coins that were being thrown at him. Swivelling round, he set off across the ticket hall, counting the coins and dividing them out between himself and his two friends, who were marching alongside him.

'The Flying Coal Trick,' said Billie. 'Always a hit.'

'I'm thinking of using two coals next time.' Harry licked his slightly burnt knuckles, and smiled. 'Obviously that might take a bit of practice.'

'Two coals or one, maybe we should include it in our stage act a bit more often.' Arthur took out his pen and notebook again, and started scribbling. 'Anyway, I still reckon we should head back to New York. But there's probably not a train back until tomorrow at least—and since we're already starting to draw crowds here, why not take advantage of that? You know how quickly word spreads. Maybe we even find a theatre, persuade them to book our act . . .'

'Good idea, Artie,' Harry said. 'Just because New York's talking about us, no reason why New Orleans can't start doing the same, eh?'

'So I guess we need a place a stay,' Arthur continued. 'Any ideas, Billie? You're the one who knows your way around, after all.'

'Sure do,' said Billie. 'That's the oddest thing of all about this business, isn't it?'

Harry and Arthur looked at her. Ahead of them were the doors leading out of the station, and Harry saw that Billie's gaze was fixed on them, and at the blurred shapes in their frosted windows, hints of the city beyond.

'Of all the places we could have ended up, who'd have thought it would be New Orleans?' Billie hurried on. 'The one place in the whole of America that I know best. This is where it all started off, guys—my long journey on the road north, just me and a bag on my shoulder to keep me company . . .'

'That's right—after your escape from the Grace Villa Orphanage.' Arthur chuckled. 'When you tied up the owner and lowered yourself out a window with a rope of knotted sheets—I've always loved that story.'

'A fair few other things happened to me before that, here in New Orleans. Some good, some not so good . . .' She pushed straight out through the doors to the station. 'Anyway, I definitely know somewhere to stay—come on!'

Harry grabbed Arthur's arm, and together they chased after her, but Billie was already halfway down the steps outside, her smock fluttering out behind her in the breeze. Harry and Arthur followed Billie out into the city, along streets unlike any others Harry had seen before.

The late-afternoon sun was fading, but every building seemed to gleam, white walls and shutters pulsing with light wherever the sun touched them. Wrought-iron balconies jutted out into the street, their intricate loops sparkling. Chains dangled from the balconies, and at the end of each one a huge flowering plant hung, the sun shining onto the purple flowers, making them glow. Harry sniffed the rich perfume wafting from the blooms. But then his nose wrinkled as he swung to the left, and followed Billie down a dark alleyway.

Sour odours drifted in the gloom. Harry felt a drip of water on his neck and he looked up to see hundreds of laundry lines criss-crossing between the rickety buildings, each one crowded with clothes attempting to dry in the humid heat. Voices, some in English, some in languages he didn't understand, floated out of broken windows, along with the sound of someone playing the piano, slightly out of tune but incredibly fast. Billie led them out of the alley, across another street and up to a low, broken-down wall. Harry looked over it and saw the huge brown river, stretching away into the distance.

'The Mississippi River.' Billie swung over the wall, and trod down some steps onto a rickety wooden wharf. 'C'mon—they're always around here this time of day.'

Harry followed her down the steps. He looked around at the vast murky river, glittering in the sun. Its far side was thick with haze, but he saw buildings, docks, and factory towers there. Steam ferries, rowing boats, and schooners ploughed the waters, along with a vessel he didn't recognize, a huge white one built out of clapboards, with a circular paddle rotating behind. Harry heard voices—high-pitched, excited ones—and saw that Billie, who had stopped halfway along the wharf, was surrounded by small, ragged children tugging her clothes and laughing.

'Billie! It is you, isn't it?'

'You came back!'

'Where have you been?'

'We always knew you'd come back one day!'

The wharf creaked as the children leapt about. More ran in, some about five years old, some younger.

Harry listened to their voices, and realized that the children had almost exactly the same accent as Billie, the same bouncing drawl. He watched them as they left Billie and ran back along the jetty towards a cluster of moored fishing boats at its end. A group of men and women were lugging baskets of fish, and the children crowded around them laughing and pointing back at Billie.

'Who are these people?' Harry asked. 'How come you've never told us about them?'

'You've told us pretty much everything else that's happened to you,' Arthur added. 'You and your stories of life on the road. Chefs in Chattanooga, blind tramps in Tennessee, sabotaged laundries in Atlantic City—'

'Some stories aren't so easy to tell.' Billie looked out across the river. 'Doesn't mean they don't matter, though. The Islanders, that's who these folk are. Come and sell their fish in the markets every day. But that's the bit of New Orleans they live in, always have done. Fisherman's Point. Right out there.'

She pointed across the river, towards the haze on the other side. Harry made out an outcrop of land, surrounded by jetties and fishing skiffs, with a collection of huts on it. Smoke rose from the huts' chimneys, darkening the haze, and Harry saw tiny shapes moving on the jetties. He heard something, and glanced back at Billie. Her eyes, he noticed, seemed strangely bright.

'They took me in,' she said. 'We'd just arrived in New Orleans, me and my Ma . . .'

'Your Ma?' Harry frowned. 'But I thought you were an orphan?'

'I am.' Billie looked at him. 'Things don't always stay the way they're meant to be, do they?'

Harry felt a blush climbing up his neck and spreading over his face. He looked down at the rickety timbers tilting under his boots. Harry felt Billie take hold of his hand and he looked up.

'It's not your fault, Harry. I've never told you this stuff—can't expect you to guess it, can I? And it happened a while ago—two years, more or less. I should be getting used to it by now.' She looked back across the river. 'We were on the road, me and Ma. We'd been doing fine, like we always did. But then Ma got sick. Real sick. The Islanders, they took us in, and they did what they could to help her. Used some of their medicines and special prayers. It wasn't enough but . . .' She managed a smile. 'At least I wasn't on my own. And I wasn't on my own afterwards, either. They told me I could stay as long as I wanted and—'

'And for a while you did.' A voice cut in. 'But only for a while.'

Harry turned, the warmth still lingering in his face. He watched Billie move away from him towards one of the Islanders, an elderly woman, with children clustered behind. Billie stepped forward and then hesitated, waiting.

'Child, you have come back.' The elderly woman spoke. 'My fears are at an end.'

She walked up to Billie, her cotton dress stirring in the breeze, her grey hair tied under a plain lace bonnet. She looked down, intricate wrinkles spreading out from her eyes. Wrinkles spread over her hands too, hands that she placed on Billie's head.

'I'm sorry, Auntie May,' Billie whispered. 'I tried to explain to you . . .'

'You did. So many times. And so many times I told you my reply. When we took you and your poor mother in that day, this home became yours. And when all was lost . . .' The old woman pushed her fingers through Billie's hair. 'Why, then our village became your home more than ever. And a home is not something to be lightly thrown away! Don't you see, L'll Billie?'

'I do . . .' Billie's voice faltered. 'But I had no choice. You hardly had enough food for your own children then and—'

'It's true, it was a difficult time. But we Islanders have known plenty of those, and we always will.' Harry noticed the old woman's eyes, just for an instant, move off in another direction, back towards the city. But then they returned to Billie. 'Somehow, we would have found a way. I told you that, plain, at the time. Not that I believed for a moment that you'd listen.'

'I beg your pardon?' Billie looked up.

The old woman was smiling. The wrinkles on her face shifted their positions, and the corners of her mouth curved upwards. Harry saw that, behind her, the other men and women were gathering, and he saw that they were smiling down at Billie too.

'A tough little customer, you've always been that.' The old woman tutted. 'It was what made me fond of you in the first place, so I can hardly complain, can I? Even if I did, you probably wouldn't listen to that either.'

'I . . . But . . .' Billie blustered.

'Don't worry, L'll Billie.' Auntie May beamed. 'You may be tough, but you'll always be true, too. Not everyone who comes across us Islanders trusts us, understands our ways, our practices. But you did. I knew you'd never forget us. And so it has proved, L'll Billie, so it has proved.'

Her arms swooped around Billie and in a single move the old woman was embracing her. Other Islanders joined and soon Billie was lost in a mass of encircling arms, and when Harry glimpsed her he saw a single tear shining on her cheek. At the same time, he realized that Arthur was touching his shoulder.

'Who would have thought she'd never have mentioned any of this?' Arthur whispered. His eyes, Harry noticed, were shining too.

'It's like she said—some stories aren't so easy to tell. She's probably been thinking about it the whole time we've known her,' Harry said. 'We might never have found out about it if we hadn't ended up here.'

'I guess so.' Arthur hesitated for a minute. 'Maybe it's that last bit that's slightly . . . strange.'

'Arthur?' Harry turned. He noticed his young friend's head was slightly tilted to the side, as he stared at Billie and the Islanders.

'It's just—what on earth is this Order of the White Crow organization up to?' Arthur tapped Harry's pocket, from which the pale green letter could just be seen, protruding. 'Knock-out drugs, locked suitcases, mysterious instructions about an investigation—not only that but it's brought us to the one city in America where Billie knows someone, cares about someone . . .' He nibbled his lip. 'What's going on, Harry?'

'I'm not sure,' Harry muttered, as he tried to puzzle out what Arthur was saying.

'To the boats!' One of the Islanders cried. 'Quickly!'
The huddle of arms flew apart. Auntie May was

staring back towards the city, a worried look on her face. Harry turned too. He heard a throb of noise echoing out from the city's buildings, screams, the pounding of boots. He felt vibrations from the din, making their way through the wharf's timbers.

'What's wrong?' Billie pulled at Auntie May's dress.

'You left us in difficult times, child. But there have never been more difficult, more terrible times for us Islanders than these.' Auntie May shook her head. 'As I have said, not everyone understands our ways . . . Come with us . . . Come back to Fisherman's Point . . .'

Two other Islanders tugged at her arm. They hurried her down the wharf towards the boats, which were a blur of untying ropes, hoisting sails. Harry saw that some of the children who had greeted Billie were shaking with fright as they scrambled into a boat and huddled in its prow. He turned round and concentrated on the terrible noise, which was even louder now.

A deafening, ugly roar.

Harry ran up the jetty. He climbed the steps three at a time, and vaulted over the wall into the street. The noise was coming from a nearby street, and he headed for it. He heard footsteps behind him, and saw Billie and Arthur following him. He waved them on, ran round the corner of the street, and froze.

Hundreds of people, surging towards him, waving placards angrily. Harry stumbled back, trying to get to the side of the street, but it was too late. The crowd swallowed him up and Harry saw the writing on the nearest placards, daubed in red.

'BANISH THE ISLANDERS!'

'THE ISLANDERS! RID US OF THEIR EVIL!'

'THROW THEM OUT! DRIVE THEM FROM OUR CITY!'

# Chapter Three

The crowd swept up the street. Craning his neck, Harry saw Billie and Arthur bobbing along further back, too far away to reach. *At least they're together.* Swinging round, he stared up at another placard. 'ISLANDERS, BE GONE.' Then he looked at the people in the crowd.

They were shouting, wailing, shaking their fists. Craning his neck again, Harry saw other people, gathered at the sides of the street and up on balconies, watching the crowd go by. Their expressions were wary; none of them made any attempt to stop the crowd, and Harry didn't blame them, feeling the strength and speed of the bodies sweeping him along. He looked back at the faces around him, which were alive with fear, determination, rage.

'What's going on?' Harry asked a man closest to him.

'Haven't you heard?' The man roared back. 'The whole city's talking about it! Those folk on Fisherman's Point, they've gone too far this time!'

'Don't tell him, he's only a boy.' A woman, her eyes peeping fearfully out from under a ribboned bonnet, bobbed past. 'Some say dark deeds like these can spread their wickedness simply by being spoken of.'

'Dark deeds?' Harry tried to keep his balance.

'Spells, hideous curses, wicked dealings with spirits! Oh, those Islanders and their terrible ways!' The fearful woman bobbed on. 'We do not wish to know of such evil . . .'

'We have no choice!' Another man, keen-eyed, and wearing the white collar of a priest. 'Mayor Monticelso didn't have a choice, did he?'

'Mayor Monticelso?' Harry asked.

'The best, the kindest mayor this city's ever had! Set up brand new hospitals! Saved whole neighbourhoods from the floods! A worthy man!' The priest swung round, and turned pale. 'Not that it did him much good! Look, look at what the Islanders have done to him! THERE HE IS!'

The crowd burst out into a square. Across it, a building loomed, ten storeys high, with marble steps leading up to bronze doors. Harry saw a horse-drawn cab wheeling up to the steps, with a coat of arms on its side. A door flew open, and liveried men stepped out, carrying a large, gilded chair, which they hoisted onto their shoulders. Tied into the chair with silken ropes was the struggling, flailing body of an elderly man, with the most terrified face Harry had ever seen.

The old man shuddered all over. His eyes bulged, his lips stretched, his teeth chattered. All the blood seemed to have drained from his face, and yet he was hideously alive, every muscle quivering. The men carried the chair up the steps, and Harry watched, and flinched. He realized that the crowd had frozen, staring as the men carried their trembling load up the steps.

'Save Mayor Monticelso!'

'Banish the Islanders!'

'Banish them! Banish them for ever!'

The crowd surged forward again, across the square, and Harry stumbled with it. The men with the chair sped up, arriving at the bronze doors and vanishing through them, but the crowd had already reached the steps and would have swept all the way up them too, had it not been for a tall, perfectly bald figure, dressed in black, who had leapt ahead. He strode up the first few steps and swung round. His arms, unnaturally long, shot out on either side of him.

'Your rage is just, my friends!' the man cried. His mouth was quite small, Harry noticed, despite the fierceness of the words flying from it. 'How can we not be driven to anger at the sight of our poor mayor, returned from hospital in this terrible state. Why, he is in the grip of a living torment. And we know who is responsible for that, do we not? Who else could it be but—'

'The Islanders! The Islanders!'

'They're the ones behind it!'

'You tell them, Dupont!'

'Oscar Dupont! You hear us, if no one else does!'

The crowd began to surge up the steps, a roar of noise. But the thin, bald man fluttered his hands, and the action seemed to hold the crowd in place. He glanced over his shoulder, and Harry saw a corner of that little mouth curve into a smile. A collection of elegantly dressed ladies and gentlemen had emerged from the bronze doors, and were nervously staring down at the crowd. At their head was a grey-haired lady who, after exchanging a few words with the others, descended the steps. Her taffeta dress rippled, and her left hand gripped a long ivory stem, at the top of which was a pair of spectacles, held in front of her eyes. Oscar Dupont waited for her to join him.

'You have heard enough from me, citizens of New Orleans,' he said with a bow. 'Madame Melrose, acting head of the council, will address you now . . .'

'*Tout à fait!* By which I mean, indeed I shall!' the lady stuttered, her voice heavy with a French accent even when she used English words. 'Citizens, I have been given the responsibility of acting head of the council during this terrible crisis. And it is on behalf of the council that I speak now.' She waved feebly up at the ladies and gentlemen by the bronze doors. '*Mais je n'ai rien de plus à ajouter*—that is to say, I have nothing further to report . . .'

'Impossible!'

'There must be something!'

'Tell us! Tell us!'

'*Silence, je vous prie.* For the sake of dear Mayor Monticelso himself.' Her spectacles wobbled on top of their stem. 'He has been brought back here to City Hall, the mayoral residence, in the hope that he will benefit from calmer, more familiar surroundings. He has lived and worked here for so many years, after all—and we have asked many of those who benefitted from his works to come and wish him well—patients at his hospitals, pupils of his schools, beneficiaries of his charitable schemes. We believe he is still conscious of his surroundings—perhaps well-wishers will stir happy memories in him of the good deeds he achieved within these walls. But how can such a plan work if all he hears is *une foule en colère,* by which I mean, an angry mob!' Her voice broke, as the crowd's cries swelled. 'Is that not true, Doctor Mincing? Why, you have been tending to him day and night!'

Madame Melrose gestured desperately at a stooped figure who was treading down the steps clutching a small leather bag. Dark rings circled his eyes, a straggling beard sprouted from his chin and he seemed even more nervous than Madame Melrose, his bag wobbling in his grip.

'I fear Madame Melrose is correct, citizens of New Orleans.' His voice wobbled too. 'There is no improvement in the patient. I can only report what is already known—that Mayor Monticelso was found collapsed at his desk three days ago. I suspected a heart attack at first, or a stroke, but I fear such theories have turned out to be somewhat . . . optimistic.' The dark-ringed eyes stared. 'Mayor Monticelso does indeed seem to be in the grip of a terrible convulsion. His body is alive, and yet his mind seems entirely out of his control. Strange nightmares seem to grip him, from which he has no escape, and they produce in him the symptoms of the most extreme fear. His muscles shake, his teeth gnash, his skin sweats profusely—nothing can relieve him. My apologies, citizens of New Orleans. I can only say that I will work day and night until I arrive at a proper medical diagnosis—'

'I wish you luck, Doctor Mincing!' Oscar Dupont's arms shot upwards again. 'But the citizens of New Orleans are beginning to reach their own understanding, medical or not.'

Harry glanced round to see every face in the crowd staring at that tall figure. He looked back and saw Doctor Mincing backing up the steps. The other ladies and gentlemen of the council edged towards the bronze doors too. Only Madame Melrose stood her ground, gripping the stem of her spectacles.

'The Islanders!' The words thundered from Oscar Dupont. 'How can anyone deny it! Them and their dark ways. For as long as anyone can remember, those folk have lived out there on Fisherman's Point—who knows when they came to New Orleans, or where they were before? But one thing we do know—their ways and practices are different from ours. Different and dreadful, too. Deadly magic, that's what they practise there in those filthy huts.' He glared at Madame Melrose. 'Deadly magic that is more than capable of reducing another human being to the state in which our poor mayor finds himself. His mind taken over by a force he cannot control! The Islanders—they're behind this terrifying act! You know that, same as I.'

'Monsieur Dupont, Citizens of New Orleans—there is no foundation to your fears!' Madame Melrose backed away. 'Why, there is no greater friend of the Islanders than Mayor Monticelso himself. Indeed, he took a special interest in them, visiting them, learning their ways; he even wrote about their unique history and culture in a small book he published. He cared for them, just as he cared for us all!'

'More fool him!' Oscar Dupont howled. 'They bewitched him, it would seem! Possibly he refused some demand of theirs, for money or for favourable treatment under the city's laws. And they have avenged themselves most swiftly. A curse, that is what they have devised. Using their magic, they have raised a spirit and set it on him. That is why he contorts so! That is why his mind and body are no longer his! A spirit lurks within him, and not just any spirit, I would wager . . .'

His arms swung even higher. The words hurtled out of that tiny mouth.

'A demon! That is what they have put upon him! A demon curse!'

'A DEMON CURSE! A DEMON CURSE!'

There was no controlling the crowd. It pushed up the steps again, and Oscar Dupont stalked at the head of it, thrusting an arm towards Madame Melrose, who shrieked and fled up the steps. But Dupont kept striding after her, and the crowd pursued her too, chasing her all the way up to the bronze doors and hammering upon them. Harry stood apart and watched the rest of the crowd race past. He recognized some of the faces from before: the fearful woman with the bonnet, the keen-eyed priest. Both of them had changed, and their expressions seemed to contain nothing but rage.

'Harry?'

Harry turned round and saw Arthur standing just beside him, red-faced, and out of breath.

'Quick! It's Billie—she heard what they're all saying . . .' He pointed into the crowd. 'About her friends. She says we've got to help them. Come on!'

Harry was already diving through the crowd, pulling Arthur along with him. He ducked under arms, dodged around shoes, and scrambled out onto the cobbles of the street. Arthur toppled out too, and together they ran off down the street leading away from the square.

Harry's gaze swung to the left. He had seen something.

The horse-drawn cab with the coat of arms was waiting at the side of the street. Its driver, wearing the same livery as the officials who had carried Mayor Monticelso up the steps, leant against the cab, smoking a pipe. Various other servants wearing the same uniform stood with him, smoking pipes too. But Harry wasn't looking at any of them.

Two men, not wearing uniform, were walking along the sidewalk. Both were scruffily dressed—one had a greasy beard shaped like a dagger, and the other a pair of darting yellowed eyes. The man with the beard was extending his arm, his fingers fluttering just next to the driver's coat.

A tiny flash of light. That was all, but Harry had seen it. He glimpsed a small bundle of keys being lifted out of the coat's pocket, their metal catching the sun, and then they were gone, buried in the dagger-bearded man's fist, as he hurried on along the street, his friend beside him. *Skilful*, thought Harry. *A quick move, even for me.*

'Harry! C'mon!' said Arthur, pulling him away. Harry stumbled after him, still trying to look at the two men, but they had turned sharply off to the left down an alleyway and disappeared. The driver and the other servants carried on talking and smoking, City Hall looming beyond them at the end of the street.

*Maybe just ordinary pickpockets*, Harry thought.

And he ran after Arthur as fast as he could.

# Chapter Four

Harry sat in the ferry boat with Arthur and Billie. He watched the boatman tug on the oars, and listened to the water drip from the wooden blades. The sun had sunk low, the river's haze darkened, but Harry could still just see the shapes of other boats in the distance, their sails fluttering, their funnels pumping out smoke. He tried to make out the names on their sides, the cargoes they carried, but the sun was sinking too quickly. Only a little light remained, and Harry used it to look at the figure that was sitting beside him in the boat.

Billie's arms were wrapped around her knees. Her lips moved silently, and her gaze remained fixed on a point in the haze. Harry made out the same outcrop of land she had shown them earlier. *Fisherman's Point.*

'Took me in,' Billie muttered. 'Cared for Ma, gave her medicine, gave her food, gave her everything.

Wasn't easy for them—they're poor fishing folk, that's all. But they're good folk too, and that's why they helped.' Her fists clenched. 'And that's why we're going to help *them*.'

The boat rowed on. Harry stared at the outcrop; its huts and jetties. He made out nets spread on the ground, upturned boat hulls glistening with tar, but as far as he could see no one was in the village, or out on the jetties. Fisherman's Point, it seemed, was deserted.

Billie paid the ferryman and they stepped out of the boat. Harry and Arthur followed Billie along a board-walk, winding through reeds. The Islanders' houses were still some distance away, and Harry looked back to see the ferryman paddling quickly off into the dusk. He kept following Billie, and weaved through the huts. One rose higher than the others and Billie headed for it. She stepped through its doorway and Arthur and Harry did the same, stepping into its dark interior.

There was a fire burning under an iron kettle that dangled from a chain. Wooden chairs were gathered around it, and Harry saw Auntie May sitting in the one closest to the fire, gently tending its flames with a stick. Around her, old men and women gathered, their faces flickering in the firelight. Harry realized that the hut was full of people, a circle of them seated round the hut's edge. He sat down next to Billie on a bench opposite Auntie May. A hot tin mug was pressed into his hands, and he lifted it to his lips.

'Welcome, Billie,' the old woman said. 'Welcome to you too, Harry and Arthur. Billie tells me that you are her friends, and so you are our friends too.' She pushed the stick into the fire. 'We Islanders are good to our friends, never mind what some may think.'

Flames leapt and the shadows of the gathered Islanders hurtled around the walls, but the Islanders themselves remained still, their eyes fixed on Auntie May. A dark look had settled on her face.

'Mayor Monticelso. Our greatest friend of all.' She lifted the stick, and pointed it at Harry. 'Why, he was sat there, right where you are now, only three days ago. Time and time again he has visited us, keen to know more of us and our ways—he has written about us in a book of history about this city of ours!' She tried to smile. 'A good man, a thoughtful one—how can we be accused of harming him? Let alone in the way of which we are accused. A demon curse! We would never do such a thing . . .'

'So what happened?' Harry asked. 'If it wasn't a demon curse, what was it? There must be some sort of explanation, surely?'

The words had flown out of him too fast, and he knew he had made a mistake. He felt his face grow warm again, as Billie's fingers dug into his wrist. *Only trying to help.* He saw every face around the circle had turned, and was staring at him.

'Why should we have to explain?' an old man sitting next to Auntie May snapped. 'It is no more to do with us than anyone else, do you not see?'

'Be calm, Brother Jacques . . .' Auntie May reached for the old man's hand. His eyes were sunken, but a fierce light blazed in their depths, and it was directed at Harry, who glanced around the hut and saw that every head was lowered with respect. He bowed his own head too.

'Friend of Billie's, you must understand our sadness in this matter.' Auntie May looked at him. 'For as long as we have lived in this city, we have suffered such accusations, you see.'

'Witchcraft! Evil-doing!' Brother Jacques' eyes still glared. 'What right do strangers have to spread lies of our practices. Many times, we have offered to explain these rituals, to make it clear that they are harmless—but no one will listen.'

He rose, and took Auntie May's stick. Fire flowered from its end as he lifted it to his face, and the flames made his wrinkles shift their shapes. He crossed to the other side of the hut, lifted the stick, and the darkness above him gleamed with curves of light. Harry saw, hanging up in the roof, hundreds of brass jars, each one intricately engraved.

'Watch this,' Billie whispered. 'It'll explain everything.'

Her fingers were still round his wrist. Harry looked at his friend, and wondered if he would have recognized her if he had just arrived in the room. Her smile was gone, her body tense, tightly held.

'Our people arrived in this city nearly one hundred years ago,' the old man said. 'We came from an island, and the village that was once our home, we have always been told, sat on a bank of land like this one, next to a river near a sea. We settled here, and made it our home—our own special neighbourhood of this great city of New Orleans. But even then, I believe, there was suspicion regarding our . . .'

'Our ways,' finished Auntie May.

Brother Jacques beckoned, and a child hurried towards him, holding a pole. Brother Jacques pointed, and the child angled the pole up into the darkness and fetched down one of the jars. The jar settled on the floor, and Brother Jacques bent over it. Harry heard shuffling noises, and he saw that everyone in the hut had moved very slightly forward.

'In each of these jars, three spirits dwell. One is from the trees; one moves upon the earth; the other belongs in the sky. We keep these spirits together, and we nourish them with what they desire.'

With a dull scrape, the jar's lid lifted. Brother Jacques drew out a tiny net bag, filled with large, blackened seeds. Next, a handful of hawks' feathers, tied together with a cord. Finally, he lifted out something pale and coiled which Harry saw was the dried skin of a snake. He heard Arthur whisper in his ear.

'Vodou. I've read about it in books, back in the New York library.' Arthur's eyes gleamed. 'It's a religion, started off in West Africa, but it's travelled to the islands of the Caribbean and it's here too, in New Orleans. Fascinating stuff, all about the spirits of nature and—'

'Vodou. That is one name for it.' Brother Jacques was putting the three items back in the jar. 'But there are many names for it, and none of them matters, for it is the spirits themselves that concern us. We offer them these items, seeds, feathers, the skin of snakes— ordinary in themselves, yet far from ordinary in their effects. Using them, we bring the spirits of the world among us and we do so with care, with respect.'

'It is no witchcraft,' Auntie May said. 'We heal the sick, we comfort the troubled, nothing more.'

'Why would we do otherwise?' Brother Jacques sealed the jar. 'We know the spirits' power. We know their power, should folk choose, to carry out curses, to inflict harm. Handled with evil intent, they *can* become demons, it is true—demons every bit as powerful as the city fears. But why would we bring amongst us such creatures when we know, more than anyone, the evil they can do?'

He lifted the jar. Harry saw engraved patterns on the brass: plants, birds, the gleaming scales of a snake. The patterns glowed as Brother Jacques slotted the jar onto the pole, and lifted it into the roof's darkness.

'Mayor Monticelso knew this.' Auntie May leant forward. 'He sat here, and he saw us at our work. He studied the ways of our people, until he knew them almost as well as we. Why, you can read it yourself— here is his book.'

It had been passed to her by another Islander, a small volume bound in red leather. *Essays On The Peoples Of New Orleans*. Arthur took it and flicked through the pages, and Harry glimpsed printed sketches of some of the items he had just seen: the seeds, the skin, the feathers. He studied them as Auntie May spoke on.

'Mayor Monticelso knew the truth. He knew that these rituals are used only for good.'

'But who will believe us?' Brother Jacques' voice cut through. 'When the mayor himself lies in the grip of this evil! An evil that has every appearance of being the work of a demon, I cannot deny it! But no demon of ours!'

'Already the city has made up its mind.' Auntie May shook her head. 'Already they rise up against us. Those who protect us will fall from power; those who attack us will be swept to power in their place. That Oscar Dupont! And how can we defend ourselves? How can we clear our name? We are the accused—no one will believe a word we say!'

'But unless the truth is discovered about what happened to poor Mayor Monticelso, our time in this city, in this village that we know so well, is short!' The old man's eyes flashed, but with a different sort of light. Harry saw tears in them. 'I know it! We will be swept away! We will be driven from our homes!'

The whole hut shook; the windows rattled in their frames. All around, the Islanders were shouting with anger, indignation, fear, and the darkness throbbed with their cries. Auntie May reached towards Billie, sitting at Harry's side.

'Oh, child!' Her arm hovered. 'What a time you have chosen to return to us! Why, I believe it is the very *end* of our time! The end of our time at Fisherman's Point! The end of our time in New Orleans!'

'Never, Auntie May—*never.*'

Billie grabbed Auntie May's hand. Then she threw

both her arms around her, embracing her. The other Islanders reached in, and once again Billie disappeared amongst their encircling arms. But Harry caught a glimpse of her face, and he saw that her jaw was tight, her eyes narrow with determination. He felt his own jaw tighten, his own eyes narrow. He turned to Arthur.

'You were right, what you said before, Artie,' he muttered. 'It's odd all right.'

'What's that, Harry?' Arthur looked up, still flicking through the pages of Mayor Monticelso's book.

Harry reached into his jacket and took out the pale green letter. He opened it up and ran a fingertip under the words that were written there. *The Order of the White Crow* . . . He scanned the rest of the letter, several times.

'Knocked-out, locked in suitcases . . . Not only that, but we arrive in a city where some of Billie's oldest and most precious friends live. Not only *that*, but we arrive here at the exact moment when those friends could do with some help. When they need their name cleared from the accusation of a mysterious crime.'

His finger moved down to the last words on the letter. He was about to read them out, but realized Arthur was saying them anyway, from memory.

'*Prepare yourselves for your first investigation* . . .'

Harry nodded. Folding the letter up, he slid it into his pocket. He put his arm around Arthur's shoulder.

'Who knows the truth about how we've ended up here?' His grip tightened around Arthur. 'But I'm glad we did.'

# Chapter Five

Harry woke up.

He made out the straw mat beneath him, and the wooden slats of the hut with the first rays of morning light gleaming through them. Smoke curled through each of those bright beams, and Harry heard the clatter of cooking pots. He breathed in the odours of coffee, rice, fried fish and, across the hut, he saw Auntie May and some of the other Islanders, crouched around the fire, stirring spoons in saucepans and chopping vegetables. Billie and Arthur were a few feet away, sleeping next to him on their own straw mats, and Harry noticed that Billie seemed a little troubled in her sleep; her breathing was fast and she seemed to be muttering something. He reached across to pull the blanket up around her, tucking it under her chin. Her breathing slowed and her face smoothed out. Harry lay back on his mat.

He gazed up at the beams of light criss-crossing above him and lifted his arm. His hand stretched towards the light, his fingers flexing, moving between the slanting rays, trying to dodge them. A favourite game—and there was no reason not to play it now.

He closed his eyes, and let the memories drift in. The sounds of the hut changed; the smells changed too. Harry detected the warm fragrance of bread, the small loaves his mother made every morning. He heard, very faintly, voices talking Hungarian, the language he had once known so well, and in amongst them he made out the low whispers of his father's voice, reciting prayers. He could see him too, his father, those tired eyes, those drawn features, and his mother's face hovered just behind, tired and drawn too.

The voices changed. There were no prayers now, only fearful mutterings, talk of money and debts which he hadn't understood back then, and made no sense to him now. Harry opened his eyes, but the memories kept hold. *Fear.* His father's lips trembled with it, his words trembled with it, and fear had trembled on through every one of the days, weeks and months that had followed. *The Scattering,* they had called it. The family had broken up, sent off across Europe to wherever there might be hope for them, which in his case had meant ending up alone in the hold of a ship sailing across the freezing grey Atlantic. Four weeks, the voyage had lasted—four weeks of filth, hunger, and sickness, followed by the cold, hard months on the streets of New York . . .

Harry squeezed his eyes shut, and then opened them as wide as he could. The memories faded, and he concentrated on his fingers, still skilfully finding their way between the rays of sun. He doubled the speed. He had invented it back then, this game—back in the Budapest slum, back in his home where the light had streamed through holes in the tiles over his bed. It had distracted him, to focus on nothing but these tiny complicated manoeuvres, these impossible challenges of dodging the light, and he had played it ever since, crouched in the hold of a ship, sitting in a rundown Manhattan boarding house. *A distraction—but it was more than that too*, he reminded himself. In a way, this little game had been the beginning of it all, of his unusual quickness and skill, of his ability to pull off the most ingenious tricks, and the thought made him lift his other hand up to the rays of sun too, so that both sets of fingers were flexing, dodging, darting. He doubled their speed again but still not a single one strayed into the light.

'Harry?'

Billie was sitting up on the straw mat, rubbing her face, and Arthur was struggling up too. Harry nodded at them both and let his hands drop. His friends were getting up and heading towards the middle of the hut, where Auntie May was serving breakfast with the other Islanders. Harry sat with them, eating fish, rice, and potato. He felt the muscles of his fingers ache from the speed with which he had played the game. But a little bit of practice would probably turn out useful, he told himself.

*For helping Billie and her friends.*

He saw Billie whispering to Auntie May. The old woman was muttering back, her face agitated, her hands grabbing at Billie's clothes. Harry tried to listen, but they were deliberately keeping their voices low, so he concentrated on eating his food instead, washing it down with a mug of the Islanders' sweet coffee. A few minutes later he followed Billie and Arthur out onto one of the jetties, and climbed down off it into a small boat. Billie's brow furrowed as her hands moved about, untying ropes, gripping the rudder.

'I never knew you were able to sail, Billie,' said Arthur, as they glided off.

'Never been in a boat together before, have we?' Billie let a rope slide a little further through her fist, and then wound it round a cleat. 'Brother Jacques taught me—it's not the sort of thing you forget.'

She looked back over her shoulder at the huts of Fisherman's Point. Then she swung back and her hands moved fast, hoisting the sail. It stretched in the wind and the boat shot through the water, Billie leaning right out over the side, balancing it with her weight, and staring ahead.

'What were you and Auntie May talking about, just now?' Harry asked.

'I was telling her our plan, that we're going to clear their name,' Billie muttered. 'And she was trying to stop me, saying it's too dangerous.'

'She could have a point,' said Arthur, looking across the river towards the buildings huddled on the other side. 'It's a sinister business, all this.'

'I told her she didn't have a choice,' Billie continued. 'None of the Islanders can investigate, can they? No one'll believe them, like Brother Jacques said! Besides, the way things are going, it's not even safe for any of them to set foot in the city . . .'

She tightened the sail. The boat picked up speed and she leant out even further, keeping it on its course. And she stayed like that, her gaze fixed on the city ahead, until they were nearly across the river, gliding towards the same jetty where Harry and his friends had first met the Islanders the previous day.

'So—how are we going to start, Harry?' Billie said.

'We've got to get into City Hall and see Mayor Monticelso for ourselves,' Harry replied. 'If we're going to put the Islanders in the clear, we've got to find out what actually *has* happened to him. Get a closer look at him, talk to the people who are looking after him, discover as much as we can. This state he's fallen into—maybe it's some terrible illness that no one knows about.'

'Unlikely,' said Arthur, taking out his notebook. 'He's been in hospital for days, remember, and looked after by doctors—they'd have come up with something by now.'

'Then maybe he's been given some kind of poison?' Harry went on. 'He's mayor of a big city; people in power have enemies, don't they?'

'Doctors would have discovered poison, too.' Billie's face was grim. 'Y'know, I can't help thinking about what Brother Jacques said last night. About how he and the Islanders use their spirit magic for good— but that others might not do the same.'

'*Handled with evil intent, they can become demons, it is true—demons every bit as powerful as the city fears.*' Arthur read out from the notes he had made. 'Yes, I've been thinking that too.'

'A real demon curse,' said Billie. 'Set upon Mayor Monticelso by who knows who . . .'

Harry said nothing. But he couldn't help tightening his grip on the boat's side. His eyes flickered shut and he saw the mayor again, that face with all blood drained from it, those struggling limbs. *His body is alive, and yet his mind seems entirely out of his control*, that was what the doctor had said . . . Could it be that he really had been taken over by some kind of dark force? He shook his head and forced his eyes open, dispelling the troubling thoughts, as the boat glided up to the jetty. Billie pulled in the sail, Arthur tied the rope to a mooring post, and they climbed out and set off into the city.

'Who knows what the truth is?' Harry said. 'But one thing's for sure: the Islanders aren't anything to do with it.'

'You're right there,' Billie agreed.

And that's what we'll prove,' finished Arthur. 'As for getting into City Hall and seeing Mayor Monticelso, I've got a plan for that too—let's pay a visit to the New Orleans Public Library, shall we?'

He set off down the street. Billie hurried after him and Harry started following too, but then noticed something, and stopped.

Another street curved off to the left. It was the same street he had run along the day before, hurrying away from City Hall with Arthur. He could make out City

Hall down at the end of it now, its roof and the tops of its pillars, but he wasn't interested in that. Instead, he focused on a point about halfway along the street, the exact same point where he had seen the driver and the other uniformed servants laughing and smoking by the cab with its coat of arms.

The two pickpockets were there.

*Daggerbeard and Yelloweyes, that's what I'll call them.* Harry saw them quite clearly, hovering in the entrance to an alleyway, the very same alleyway into which they had ducked after carrying out their snatch. He remembered the bundle of keys, its metal flashing in the sun, and he could see Daggerbeard's hand was clutching something. He saw that Yelloweyes was holding something too, a small sack. It hung from his hands, and both men were peering into it. Yelloweyes' fingers gripped the sack's opening, making it twitch, and his mouth twitched too as he muttered to Daggerbeard, who was nodding. Both men, Harry noticed, kept swivelling their heads and glancing up in the direction of City Hall.

'Harry?'

'Come on, we've got to get started!'

Harry looked round. A short distance away, Arthur and Billie were waiting, Arthur holding his notebook and pen, Billie waving him on.

*Pickpockets, thieves, that's all they are. Probably nothing to do with it.*

And he ran after his friends.

Harry sat next to Billie on a bench in the marble entrance hall of the New Orleans Library. Fans turned overhead, sending air spiralling downwards. Over by the reception desk Arthur was finishing his conversation with the librarians, who handed him a slip of paper, which he signed. Stuffing it into his pocket, he walked back towards his friends.

'Easily done,' he said. 'Thanks to being a member of the New York Public Library, I managed to get a special pass here. Put you two on it too, as guests. The newspapers are up on the fourth floor: the *New Orleans Post*, the *Louisiana Mail*, everything.'

He led them up a flight of steps. Pushing through some double doors, he swept into one of the reading rooms, a domed space with gleaming desks, and set off along one of the aisles of bookshelves. Harry and Billie followed, the spines of thousands of books flashing past. Harry smiled as he watched Arthur swing his arms and click his fingers happily as he walked. Halfway down the aisle, the tweed-suited boy even paused to tug out a couple of books and, after studying them with interest, tucked them under his arm.

'Feeling at home, are we?' Harry asked, as Arthur hurried on towards a spiral staircase.

'Absolutely. Apart from anything else, they use the same classification system as the New York library, and I know that pretty much backwards.' Arthur reached the top of the staircase, hurried off down another corridor, and thudded through a teak door. 'Anyway— let's get to work.'

They were in the Newspaper Room, and Arthur walked straight over to the huge ledgers on the shelves. Pulling one down, he tottered across the room with it, and Harry saw that it contained bound copies of newspapers. He ran across to the shelves too, and pulled down more ledgers, slamming them onto the table next to Arthur. Dust billowed, but Arthur could just be seen opening the ledgers, flicking through the pages, scanning the endless columns of print. Sliding out the leather notebook, he placed it open on the table and started making notes on it with his fountain pen.

'Anything to do with Monticelso, that's what we need. Particularly stuff about his kind, charitable deeds. Madame Melrose said they want people that the mayor's helped to come and see him, didn't she? Wish him well, stir happy memories. It's just a question of who those people are going to be . . . Bother this pen!' He held up the pen, which was dribbling ink. 'It's been leaking more and more ever since we got here. I'm wondering it's the humidity. An increase in atmospheric pressure can have that effect, apparently.' He turned back to the newspaper. 'Anyway, let's see—ah!'

Harry and Billie leaned over Arthur's shoulder. Arthur's finger was planted directly by an article half-way down a page, and he was reading it through, while his free hand made more spattering purple notes.

'*Yesterday, here in Biloxi Valley, Mayor Monticelso of New Orleans City made another visit to the Tobermory Swamp School, a school for orphaned children from the impoverished area.* Sounds promising . . .' The finger tapped the page. '*Presenting a cheque from city funds, he spoke of how continued support for the children at the school was vitally needed*— Right, that'll do. I think we can pass ourselves off as orphans from a swamp, can't we?'

Harry looked at Billie. She was looking at him too, and he saw the smile on her face. Together they turned and studied their friend, standing before them in his neatly tailored tweed suit.

'What?' Arthur asked.

'We'll sort you out,' said Harry.

Ten minutes later, back in the New Orleans sun, the door of a junk shop slammed behind them. Arthur walked to the window of the shop next door, and adjusted his new clothes: a pair of worn-out trousers and a mould-covered jacket. He slid his note-book and pen into a frayed pocket and Harry handed him a knapsack with his tweed suit stuffed inside. Billie bent over the gutter, lifted up a handful of mud, and gave Arthur's trousers a few smears.

'We're not just street kids, we're swamp kids. Meant to have walked all the way in from Biloxi too, which would mean crossing a marsh or two.' She gave herself a smear too. 'Got to look the part. Reminds me of the time I actually did get lost in a swamp, the Okefenokee Swamp, out Georgia way. Nasty boggy place and then there were the alligators—'

Harry chuckled. It had been some time, by Billie's standards, since she had last told them one of her tales of the road, and it was good to hear her chattering away again. He listened to her as she led them along another street with iron balconies and hanging baskets of blooms. Harry breathed in the rich perfume of the flowers, and followed her around the corner. Then he realized Billie had stopped talking. He looked up ahead, and saw why.

Ahead of them was City Hall. And marching towards it, just a few feet away from them, was Oscar Dupont.

He was heading towards the crowd. It was even bigger than the day before, gathered around the

City Hall steps. For the moment it seemed calm, and Harry wondered if it perhaps had just returned to wish the mayor well. *But it won't be calm for long*, he thought, as he watched Oscar Dupont march towards it, assistants hurrying behind him. Under his arm the politician carried a sheaf of papers, on which Harry glimpsed scribbled handwriting. *Another speech.* He saw that Dupont's mouth was twitching, shaping the words he intended to deliver, and up on his bald head, a pulse twitched too, as he quickened his pace.

And marched straight into Billie, who had thrown herself into his path.

'Don't you dare say that stuff again! Lies! It's nothing but lies!'

'Billie!' Harry grabbed her arm and hissed in her ear. 'We're meant to be pretending to be swamp kids, remember?'

He tried to pull her back. *Getting into City Hall, that's all that matters for now.* But it was too late. Oscar Dupont had stopped and was studying Billie, and Harry and Arthur too. Not a trace of surprise could be seen on his face, despite the loudness of Billie's cry.

'Lies, young lady? A serious accusation. One that I firmly refute.' He lifted an arm and pointed at the crowd. 'And a great many would agree with me.'

'Only because you've whipped them up! Got them in a frenzy!'

'More accusations and, again, I refute them. I have used only the most reasoned argument when discussing this matter.' Oscar Dupont smiled. 'I shall go further—without my speeches, without these opportunities to discuss this business peacefully, I believe the folk of New Orleans would be forced to express themselves in far more violent ways. Although I cannot guarantee, if the council continue to refuse to listen to my reasoned arguments, that there will not be violence nonetheless . . .'

Billie lunged forward. Harry pulled her back again, but already he could see several faces in the crowd turning towards them, and noticing what was going on. *Get her away.*

'Young lady, perhaps you should stay and hear me speak? You might understand better then.' Dupont looked Billie up and down. 'You would be entirely welcome, as are all good folk of New Orleans. The folk of Fisherman's Point, those are the ones we hold responsible for the demon curse. No one else has anything to fear in this great city of ours . . .'

Words poured out of Billie. Harry knew that, because he could feel them spluttering against the palm of his hand, clasped over her mouth. *Concentrate on the plan,* he told himself, as he and Arthur dragged Billie towards the City Hall steps.

But he couldn't stop his own face from twitching with anger as he glanced back at Oscar Dupont, who was laughing, tapping his sheaf of papers, and approaching his crowd.

# Chapter Six

The City Hall lobby was like the library's but higher, cooler. Uniformed officials bustled, and several of them turned in the direction of Harry, sat on a cushioned bench in his mud-smeared clothes. They were wrinkling their noses, and Harry wondered if the plan to make themselves as dirty as possible had gone a little too far, but then he glanced across to the reception counter, and saw that Arthur was already making progress.

'We're here from the Tobermory Swamp School . . . Walked all yesterday through the marsh . . . We've heard about Mayor Monticelso . . . Well-wishers . . . If it would help . . . '

*Nice work.* He was even doing a good job at changing his voice so that it sounded more like Billie's with its drawls and twangs, rather than his own clipped English accent. Satisfied, Harry turned back to Billie, who was pacing up and down, her fists clenched tightly by her sides.

'Sorry about losing it, Harry.' She mumbled the words out through gritted teeth. 'It's just when I saw him, about to say all those things again . . .'

'Don't worry.' Harry kept his voice calm and quiet. 'We'll stop Dupont, just you see. But we need to follow the plan we've agreed. Get in to see the mayor, discover what we can about this demon curse. And then we'll investigate.'

'*Mais oui*, the Tobermory School!'

Harry looked up. Arthur was still waiting at the reception desk, various officials still muttering, but a familiar voice could be heard through an open door behind the counter. Madame Melrose bustled out, addressing the officials who hurried behind her.

'One of the mayor's favourite causes. I myself have accompanied him there! Children from a school such as that—they are the sort of visitor we require, *exactement!*'

Her spectacles swung up on their ivory stalk as she inspected Arthur, and then swivelled towards Harry and Billie across the hall. She even performed a curtsey, the embroidered hems of her petticoats spreading over the marble.

'The goodness of Louisiana's citizens! Three orphans, journeying through swamp to do what they can for our noble mayor.' She swept towards them. 'You come not a moment too soon. Mayor Monticelso grows worse. Whatever help your good wishes may do, whatever happy memories they might stir, we must attempt it at once! *Suivez-moi, mes enfants*—come!'

Billie, Arthur, and Harry hurried after her. The lady's skirts fluttered and her sequin-studded shoes flashed as she led them up several flights of stairs and then down a corridor. Doors and windows flew past. Stairways rose, more corridors slanted at angles. Harry noted each detail as they walked, memorizing it, working out the shape of the huge building through which they were climbing, constructing a map in his mind. Following Madame Melrose up another flight of stairs, he glanced down another corridor and noticed two servants standing by a small wire shutter in the wall. As Harry watched, one of them opened the shutter and the other carefully loaded a pile of books and ribboned documents into a little lift inside. They closed the shutter, turned a crank on the wall, and the books and documents were winched upwards.

*A dumb waiter*, thought Harry. He noticed others, positioned on the various corridors and landings he was passing.

'Not a moment too soon, *mes enfants*.' Madame Melrose crossed to a window and looked down on the square below. Her shoulders sank. 'I fear the numbers of well-wishers has been declining—many of the people of New Orleans have decided to assist with the situation in more unpleasant ways. *Ecoutez donc!* By which I mean, just listen to them.'

The window's panes trembled with the noise outside. Harry looked down ten storeys below, to the crowd on the steps. Cries rose up from it and, jabbing through them, Harry heard the voice of Oscar Dupont addressing the mob, his papers clutched in his hand, words shooting from his tiny mouth at speed. Harry frowned, and he saw that Arthur was frowning too. Further along, Billie's whole face was clenched, but her lips were sealed shut and she wasn't saying a word.

'The distress Mayor Monticelso must feel!' Madame Melrose shook her head. 'To hear, with what little consciousness he has, the sound of the poor Islanders accused of being behind his affliction. I too know the Islanders; I too have acquainted myself with their customs—to think they would do such a thing, *c'est impossible!* They are good citizens of New Orleans! As for Oscar Dupont, stirring up such rage . . . why, that man thinks only of his own rise to power. A seat on the council, that is what he desires.' She pushed away from the window. 'This way, *mes enfants!*'

The journey continued. The noise of the crowd faded as Madame Melrose hurried up a final flight of stairs and then arrived at a carved door, in front of which two officials stood. They bowed and opened the door. Madame Melrose stepped through and went over to a stooped figure clutching a stethoscope.

'Doctor Mincing, how is our patient?'

The doctor seemed even more exhausted than the day before. His grey hair drooped, dark rings circled his eyes, the stethoscope leapt in his trembling hand. Madame Melrose beckoned towards Harry and his friends. Billie and Arthur took a step forward, but stopped, and Harry couldn't help hesitating too. He too had seen something on the other side of the oak-panelled room, just visible beyond Madame Melrose and the doctor.

A four-poster bed. Trussed onto it with silken ropes, a shuddering shape.

'Doctor Mincing agrees that it is worth a try.' Madame Melrose beckoned again. 'Mayor Monticelso was most fond of *les enfants* at the Tobermory Swamp School.'

'I will introduce you—you need to do nothing other than stand at his side.' Doctor Mincing tottered towards the bed. 'The chances of it helping are slim, but the same applies to any other medical treatment, it seems. Nothing has worked, nothing . . .' He pointed towards an oil painting on the wall. 'You seem nervous. May I suggest that you prepare yourselves by seeing Mayor Monticelso as he once was? It may console you . . . before seeing how he has changed.'

Harry walked over to the painting of an elderly man with a kindly gleam in his eyes. Ermine-lined robes were draped around his frame, a golden chain hung from his shoulders, and yet it was that gentle face that shone most clearly out of the painting. Harry looked up at it for quite some time, and then felt Doctor Mincing's hand tugging at his arm. He turned. A cold wave swept through him. He walked over to the quaking bed.

'As I say,' whispered Doctor Mincing, 'he is somewhat changed.'

The mayor's face shook all over. A taut rope ran across the forehead, holding it still, but nothing could be done about the face itself, a quivering blur. Harry wondered if there was a single muscle in it that wasn't struggling. Lips arched, flecks of sweat raced over the skin and worst of all were Mayor Monticelso's eyes, stretched wide with fear. Further down, his mouth was wide open too, but with only hoarse gasps wafting out. Harry tried to swallow, but his mouth was too dry. *A real demon curse*—staring down at this face, it seemed entirely possible.

'*Ne craignez rien, mes enfants.*' Madame Melrose stood across the bed. 'Do not be afraid, I mean. We wish your presence to reassure our mayor, to remind him of the good he has done, of the affection with which he is regarded. To surround him with frightened faces will not do—am I not right, Doctor Mincing?'

'Certainly. Further pictures of terror are the last thing the patient needs.' Doctor Mincing pushed his stethoscope between the buttons of the mayor's shirt. 'Mayor Monticelso? We have visitors for you. Children from the Tobermory Swamp School, do you recall? They have come to wish you well.'

The ropes groaned. All down the bed, ropes crisscrossed the mayor's body and they were under great strain, holding him still. Harry looked back at the face and saw, fleetingly, a flicker of the kindly expression in the painting cross those terrified features. Mayor Monticelso's lips arched, shaping a word. Harry leant close, trying to hear it, but it was gone, and the old man's face had been taken over by shaking again, his eyes bulging as if trying to struggle free, only to sink back again.

'Lost utterly in his torment!' Doctor Mincing lifted away the stethoscope, which shook almost as violently as the ropes on the bed. 'Yet another technique of modern medicine has failed!'

'And if Doctor Mincing cannot help him, who can?' Madame Melrose dropped into a chair. 'He is the most experienced of doctors, *mes enfants*. For years he has travelled around, researching every disease of the mind—have you not, Doctor?'

'Indeed I have,' said the doctor. 'I have studied in hospitals all over the world. I have undertaken dangerous field trips—why, I have even ventured into the jungles of Costa Rica in search of rare medicines for the mind. But in all my years of study, I have never seen a patient in the grip of a condition quite so cruel. It really is as if some demonic force has made its home within his mind and is devouring it from within—although such a thing is medically unheard of, naturally.'

'For such a good man to be trapped in this evil condition—*intolerable*!' Madame Melrose indicated a door, ajar but with a red ribbon tied across it. 'Why, even at the very moment of the attack he was engaged in charitable acts. He was through there, in his office. Attending to the paperwork concerning his noble endeavours and—'

'Who found him?' Harry asked. He was still unsteady from the terrible sight, but he managed to adjust his angle and peer through the door into the office. He made out scattered papers, a desk and, just visible, the edge of a wire-grille shutter on a wall.

'Clerks heard the cries from down the corridor! I was here within minutes, followed by the other councillors. We saw him collapsed behind his desk, in the grip of this terrible fit, the papers of his good work thrown into the air by his convulsions.' Madame Melrose shook her head. 'A fearful scene, and one that largely remains. The New Orleans police wish to inspect it again, but what will they discover that has not been discovered before? There is no medical explanation for this condition, and there is no other explanation for it either! *C'est un mystère!*'

'A mystery, Madame Melrose means. And one that will be with us for some time.' Doctor Mincing wound the stethoscope in his hands. 'I observe no change at all in the patient. Even if he does awaken, his mind may have been irreparably damaged after enduring such agonies. Worse, he might simply remain in this state, a perpetual victim of appalling suffering.'

The ropes strained against the body; Mayor Monticelso's face blurred into even more agonized shapes. Doctor Mincing unwound his stethoscope again but his hands shook so much that it writhed like a tormented snake. He threw himself over the patient.

'The cruelty of this torment! Madame Melrose, our words have stirred his horrors into even more terrible life!'

'The very opposite of our intention!'

'Thank goodness that it is time for his daily treatment! The one thing that seems to calm him a little, here and at the hospital—a steam bath.'

'Are the orderlies ready to take him down?'

'They will be here presently, with the wheelchair and more ropes. I impressed upon them the importance of punctuality.'

'Then leave us, *mes enfants*!' Madame Melrose pushed Harry and his friends across the room. 'I too must depart—indeed I am already late—I have a vital meeting with the Islanders.'

'The Islanders?' Billie asked.

'To discuss how best to protect them at this terrible time. But I fear little can be done. Just as little has been done here! Forgive us, *mes enfants*!' She gave them a final push out into the corridor. 'Find your way down to the lobby—a clerk awaits you there.'

The door slammed shut. Harry's mouth was still dry, and he made himself swallow. He walked along the corridor and down some stairs with his friends. Arthur brushed against him, and he saw that his friend's hands were unsteady as he fished his notebook and pen from his pocket, trying to make a few notes, the results even more splattering than usual. But it was Billie who seemed truly disturbed.

'Impossible . . . A thing like that . . .' She glanced back and steadied herself against the wall. 'The Islanders—they'd never do anything like it!'

'Of course not, but something's happened, and something pretty nasty too,' Arthur said. 'Even the doctor said it looks like "some demonic force". He certainly didn't have any other explanation, did he?'

'Doesn't mean there isn't one to find,' Harry said. They had reached the bottom of the stairs, and he saw the shutter of another dumb waiter. He stopped, checking the map in his mind.

'LOOK!' Billie cried.

She had reached a window at the end of the corridor. It was the same window they had passed on the way up, but its panes were shaking even more violently. Harry joined her, and looked down at the crowd again. It was huge, sprawling all over the steps, and it seemed to be gathering even more people from the surrounding streets, adding to its mass. Oscar Dupont was still delivering his speech, and his bald head tilted back, allowing Harry to see that tiny mouth curving in a grin. *Those who protect us will fall from power; those who attack will take their place . . .* All around Dupont Harry saw the crowd's faces white with rage and, down at his sides, he felt his hands tighten into fists.

'*They've* got an explanation, that's for sure!' Billie jabbed a finger towards the crowd. 'Down there, they think they've got it worked out, nice and simple! A demon curse put on him by the Islanders, that's all they're thinking—and how's anyone going to prove them wrong? Look at that crowd! It's twice the size already! More people joining the whole time! Who knows what they'll do, if that Oscar Dupont keeps driving them on—Harry, what are you doing?'

Harry had run over to the dumb waiter. Deep in his chest, he felt his heart quicken and tiny flickers creeping over his body, making their way all over his skin. *Good.* He often felt these sensations before one of his tricks, and it made sense that he was feeling them now, as he prepared for the task ahead. *A little nervousness is a good thing—it helps with concentrating, with focusing the mind . . .*

He worked quickly, opening the wire shutter and peering into the polished wooden box inside. He turned the crank on the wall, the box lowered, and he saw the chain from which it hung, and the empty shaft lined with pulleys and ropes. He put his head in, and peered up. A narrow tunnel of darkness led upwards and, towards the top of it, Harry made out a glimmer of light. *The shutter in Mayor Monticelso's office, three floors above.*

'Harry, didn't you hear Billie? What are you doing?' Arthur asked. 'That's a dumb waiter—it's meant for transporting cups of tea and trays of dinner and—'

'And the odd other thing.' Harry pushed his head in further, and then wriggled his shoulders into the darkness too.

'It's too small for you!' Billie's voice echoed after him. 'Anyway, we're meant to be heading down to the lobby.'

'There's a clerk waiting for us and everything!' Arthur's voice echoed too.

'Tell them I got lost.' Harry couldn't help smiling in the darkness.

And he pulled the rest of himself into the narrow shaft, closed the shutter behind him with a boot, and scrambled upwards.

# Chapter Seven

'Harry?'

Billie's and Arthur's voices kept echoing up through the darkness. Harry kept scrabbling, his boots and fingers finding holds. He gripped brackets, pulleys, ropes. Cement crumbled as he dug his fingernails between bricks. Sucking in lungfuls of dusty air, he tilted his head back and stared up.

He could see that faint glow of light, three floors above. He peered, and saw criss-crossed shadows, the sign of a metal grille. He thought back over everything he had observed, checking that he had pieced together his map of the building correctly, that he was heading for the right place. He kept climbing, digging his fingers deeper into the brickwork of the shaft, only for a clump of clement to fall away, so that he slipped.

He shot down through the dark. He flailed at the shaft's sides, tearing skin from his hands, but his boots found a hold, and he jolted to a halt. His muscles shook; sweat crawled through the roots of his hair. *Concentrate.* Brick dust kept showering down on top of him, and he winced as it entered his mouth, coating his tongue. But he was already climbing again, finding new holds, making his way up the shaft.

He stared at the brickwork. He thought about how, just a few inches away from his fingertips, uniformed servants and council men would be hurrying past smoothly plastered walls, with no idea about the small, dust-covered figure on the other side. *Unseen, unknown, just like a trick*—the thought gave him a new jolt of strength and he picked up speed, pulling, tugging, levering himself upwards until his head drew level with the wire shutter. It was latched on the other side, but Harry easily wiggled a finger through the mesh and flicked the latch. The shutter rattled up and Harry tumbled into the office, brushing brick-dust from his clothes.

His boots sank into a deep-pile rug. He breathed in the air, fresh and clean after the shaft, but still heavy with odours of leather and polished wood. The curtains of the office were drawn, but they glowed with light, the New Orleans sun blazing through their thick threads. Harry made out the door on the other side of the room, still ajar, and with the red ribbon running across it. Keeping to the shadows, he peered into the room beyond, the room in which he had just been.

*'He is secure! The ropes will hold!'*

*'The steam chamber! Down in the mayoral bathroom!'*

*'Perfumed steams will envelop him, pinioned though he may be! This way, gentlemen!'*

The voices floated through the gap in the door. Harry saw several orderlies trundling a wickerwork wheelchair towards the door. Tied into it with more ropes was the trembling mayor, wearing a cotton bathgown. The wheelchair swept out, followed by Doctor Mincing and Madame Melrose. A door slammed and the room fell quiet. Harry swivelled around and started searching the office.

*The tiniest trace, the tiniest sign.* As his eyes flicked about, Harry remembered the New York magicians he had watched, time and time again—how a barely noticeable bulge in a sleeve or flutter of a finger had revealed their secrets to him, taught him tricks. He crouched down, scanning the office, which was in exactly the state Madame Melrose had described. Papers everywhere. A few of them still lay on a mahogany desk, but the rest had been hurled all over the room, along with ledgers, books, and split-open files. Harry checked a few of the papers. Letters to hospitals, orphanages, charities. He crept round the desk, to where a chair lay tipped back. Next to it, there was a patch of papers that were crushed into the rug. Harry saw that the patch formed the shape of a human body, its arms and legs outstretched.

*This was where he lay.* Harry crouched over the crumpled documents. He saw other damaged papers at various points around the room. *Thrown there by the thrashing arms, perhaps?* He carried on examining the human shape, picking up each of the papers. As he lifted one of them he noticed a pen.

He picked it up. It was an ebony fountain pen, similar to Arthur's although with a gleaming gold nib, and not remotely leaky. It was just the pen itself—there was no sign of the lid. Harry lifted more papers, searching for it. He crouched down, scanning the surrounding rug, but there was still no sign of it. *Odd*—but then he saw it; a tiny gleaming shape nestled beside the carved foot of a chaise longue, right on the other side of the room.

He walked across and picked the lid up. It too was ebony, its metalwork gold. He rotated it in his fingers, and stared back at the pen itself. *Fifteen feet away at least.* He trod back to the desk and mimed the business out, holding the lid in his hand and swinging it round, trying to calculate the speed that would be required to throw the lid as far as the chaise longue. *Very fast indeed.* Still, the mayor had been in the grip of a fit, so it was quite possible. Harry trod back to the chaise longue, replaced the lid where he'd found it, and searched around in the glowing light for another, more useful clue. And then his head turned so fast that the muscles in his neck hurt.

*Not a clue. But something worth noticing.*

A faint chime of metal against metal. Harry glanced around, tracing the sound to the far side of the office, where there was another door. He heard the noise again, more chiming, and knew what it was. *Keys, jangling on a ring.* He waited, and heard a different noise, a far more alarming one.

A key, digging into the lock.

Harry stumbled back across the room. He heard the key turn, the mechanisms of the lock's insides grinding. He heard the latch spring just as he was scrambling back into the dumb waiter shaft. The door opened and he dropped down into the darkness, holding onto the edge of the hatch. He braced his boots against the bricks, keeping his eyes just at the level of the hatch, allowing him to peer back into the office.

Two figures edged into the room, shrouded in shadow. But Harry had already seen enough to recognize them.

A dagger beard. And two yellowed eyes.

# Chapter Eight

The two men edged into the room. For the first time, Harry saw them close up. Their clothes were old and scruffy, their faces dirty, their hair full of grease. Daggerbeard was thicker set, and he kept himself in front of Yelloweyes, who was a scrawny figure, a thick scar curving down one of his cheeks. Daggerbeard carried a ring of keys, swinging from a finger. *Must be the ones he stole.*

'Are they gone?' Yelloweyes whispered, staring across the office towards the door of the mayor's bedroom.

'Of course, that's what we heard the servants saying, wasn't it?' Daggerbeard pocketed the keys. 'Steam treatment at noon, every day.'

'Then let's finish the job off,' muttered Yelloweyes, as he held up the sack.

It hung from his hand as they headed for the door. Harry noticed that he was holding it some distance from his body as he edged across the room. Carefully, the two men stepped around the scattered papers, pushed open the door and stepped over the red ribbon that ran across it. Harry waited, and then pushed himself upwards so that he was leaning slightly out of the shaft, and able to get a better view. His boots dug into the brickwork, his fingers gripped the hatch's edge, and he felt his muscles ache from the effort of holding the position. But, like that, he was able to see through the open door into the next room, and glimpse what the men were doing.

They were standing over Mayor Monticelso's bed. The body was gone; only ropes and rumpled bedding remained. Yelloweyes dangled the sack over where the Mayor had been, his scar altering its shape as a smile formed on his face. Daggerbeard crouched down and peered at the floorboards just beneath the bed. He rummaged in his pocket and took out a small chisel. He glanced up at Yelloweyes, who stood there waiting with the sack.

'The spot . . .'

'Finish it . . .'

'Put it under the floorboards . . .'

'Let it do its work . . .'

Daggerbeard dug the chisel's tip between two of the boards beneath the bed. He levered, and the nails gave.

Harry leaned even further forward, craning his neck, and saw the end of a floorboard lifting. Yelloweyes was crouching down now too, the sack still in his hand. Daggerbeard's breathing grew laboured as he tugged at the chisel, steadily levering the floorboard higher. Yelloweyes was opening the sack and peering inside. Harry kept watching and, as he did so, he remembered what Brother Jacques had said, and what his friends had said too, in the boat earlier that day.

*A real demon curse . . . Set upon Mayor Monticelso by who knows who . . .*

He lost his foothold, and slipped.

Brickwork crumbled, rattling away down the shaft. Harry slithered back down into the hatch, but felt a sharp pain in his back, and jolted to a halt. His eyes were level with the bottom of the hatch, and he saw, through the doorway, that the two men had spun round. He tried to wriggle down inside the hatch, out of view, but he couldn't, and the pain increased when he tried. Reaching a hand behind himself, he discovered that his jacket had snagged on one of the pulley mechanisms, and a fold of skin was trapped with it. He tried to struggle free, but then froze as he saw Daggerbeard appear in the doorway to the office.

Harry's eyes, trapped at the level of the hatch, stared at the bulky figure, who was no longer holding the chisel. Instead, he was sliding a very different tool from one of his sleeves.

*A heavy iron hook, nearly a foot long.*

'It was in here.' Daggerbeard muttered over his shoulder.

'Well check it out then—and be quick about it!' Yelloweyes called back.

The hook's point was jagged, and it gleamed in the light. Daggerbeard gripped it in his fist as he scanned the room. Yelloweyes joined him and together the two men's heads turned, their gaze moving steadily round the office. Harry tried to stay as still as possible, but he knew the top half of his head was in view. The shadows protected him, but that was all. His whole body shook; sweat gathered in his clothes. He watched the gaze of the two men move steadily towards him. The hook in Daggerbeard's hand, he noticed, was being raised . . .

'Come with me, gentlemen! I have need of further equipment; I will show you what to bring.'

Daggerbeard and Yelloweyes spun round. Mincing's voice could be heard, and footsteps too, pounding nearer. The hook vanished back up Daggerbeard's sleeve and the two men were racing back into the mayor's bedroom. Harry started struggling to free himself of the pulley, but he could still see into the next room. Daggerbeard was snatching up his chisel; Yelloweyes prised at the floorboard, trying to push the sack through the gap, but it wouldn't fit. The footsteps were even closer now, and, with a growl of frustration, Daggerbeard stamped down on the board and pulled Yelloweyes after him. They thundered back through the paper-strewn office and were gone, their hunched shapes vanishing through the door at the end of the room. Back in the mayor's bedroom Doctor Mincing could be heard bursting back in.

*'Quickly, gentlemen! Follow me!'*

Harry finally unsnagged himself and scrambled downwards, his boots and hands finding holds. Cement crumbled around him, but there was no danger of being discovered now, and he doubled his speed. Once again, he stared at the brickwork of the shaft, and thought about the smoothly plastered rooms and corridors on the other side, and about how, somewhere amongst those rooms and corridors, two men would be racing along, making their escape with their stolen keys and mysterious sack. *Find them.* Peering down, he made out the faint glow of the next hatch, and he scrambled even faster until he reached it, and swung straight out. Collapsing onto the rug, he bounced up immediately, brushed cement, dust and some bits of rubble from his clothes, and then ran down staircases and corridors until he reached the front lobby. Skidding across the marble floor, he slammed straight out through the front doors and onto the steps. He ran straight down them, past Oscar Dupont and his chanting mob, and headed across the square to where Billie and Arthur were waiting for him.

'Nice of you to join us.' Billie tutted, as he stumbled up. 'Just like you, running off without saying what you're doing and—'

'Did you see them come out?'

'Who?'

'Them! The men!' Harry struggled for breath. 'A beard like a dagger . . . Two yellowed eyes . . . I saw them before . . . They—'

'Harry, are you all right?' Arthur clutched his arm.

'We need to follow them. You go round and watch the front, Artie. I'll check round the side and see if there are any other doors . . .' He tried to keep talking, but had to suck in more air. 'Billie, you run round the other way and—'

'A beard like a dagger? Two yellowed eyes? I don't suppose that's them, right there?'

'QUICK! FOLLOW ME!' cried Harry.

The two mysterious men were hurrying down a nearby street. Harry raced after them, Billie and Arthur running along beside him. He ran across the street, swerving past a cart, but the men were too far ahead, disappearing amongst the crowds.

'Let Billie do this!' Arthur spluttered. 'She's the one who knows her way round New Orleans, doesn't she?'

Billie had already swerved off, darting down an alleyway. She leapt over a garbage can, ran around a corner and, when Harry caught her up at the alley's end, he looked out to see Daggerbeard and Yelloweyes hurrying down a different street, but much closer than before.

'Nice shortcut, Billie!'

She was already running up a fire escape. Harry climbed after her, Arthur following too, and a minute later they were stalking along the flat roofs of the street's buildings, keeping their eyes on the two men, clearly visible amongst the people below. Harry's breath was back, and the story of what he had seen in Mayor Monticelso's office burst out of him as they marched past chimney stacks, and leapt between roofs.

'You think they're behind it, Harry?' Arthur asked.

'Of course they're behind it! Who knows if it's a demon curse or not—but whatever it is, they're doing it! Why else would they be trying to bury something right under the bed where he's lying?'

'But what was it?' Billie demanded. 'Why were they putting it down there?'

'Don't know.' Harry leapt onto the next roof. 'That's why we've got to follow them, find out who they are.'

'Fair enough, but it's a good thing that we can follow them from up here,' said Arthur. 'If you're right, and they did do something that caused Mayor Monticelso to end up in the state he's in . . . Well, I'm just saying it's sensible to follow at a safe distance. We could be talking about men wielding a dark magical curse, after all— actually, that seems extremely likely, if you ask me.' He swallowed, and kept walking. 'Then there's the hook you told us about. How big was it again?'

'They're heading for the river, Billie! Look!' cried Harry, pointing at the men, who were swerving off in a new direction. But Billie was already darting across the roof. Reaching another fire escape, she ran down it with her friends. Halfway down, Harry saw Daggerbeard and Yelloweyes reach a low wall, jump over it, and run out along a wharf. A tangle of moored boats floated beside it. The two men got into one of the boats, a skiff, and cast the rope loose. With the flick of an oar, they were heading out onto the Mississippi, a sail already racing up the skiff's mast and catching the wind.

'Follow me,' said Billie.

Jumping off the bottom step of the fire escape, she ran down an alleyway and took a shortcut through a graveyard filled with white-washed tombs. They burst out through the gate, hopped over another wall, and Harry saw their own boat waiting at its wharf. They leapt into it and, with a push of an oar, they were out onto the river.

The sail rustled up. Billie's hands raced around the boat's ropes even faster than they had before, and foam churned up around the boat's prow as it gathered speed. She gripped the rudder with one hand and, with the other, pointed ahead to where, further up the river, the skiff with the two men could be seen. Harry tried to make it out more clearly, but the light was fading and he looked up to see that, out of nowhere, grey clouds were swelling in the sky, blotting out even the New Orleans sun. Gloom spread over the river. Harry heard thunder rumble, and he saw the clouds' edges flicker and grow dark again.

The boat sailed on. The clouds kept swelling, and a fine rain fell from them, coating Harry's clothes and skin with tiny droplets. He wiped them away, but they gathered again. Up ahead, he saw the skiff with the two men alter its course and head for a muddy stretch of shoreline where a rickety boathouse was built on stilts over the river.

The skiff's sail lowered. The two men, tiny shapes in the distance, splashed into the water and pulled the boat up onto the mud. They hurried up some steps and disappeared into the boathouse. Harry made out other boats clustered nearby. Almost all of them, he noticed, had fishing nets piled in them.

'What is this place, Billie?' Arthur whispered.

'Can't say,' Billie replied. 'We're quite a way down the river. I've heard they're fishing folk down this way—guess that's what these men are too. I suppose that would make sense of that massive, jagged iron hook you saw . . .'

'Although they're not *just* fishermen, that's for sure—not from what you've told us.' Arthur's face was pale and tense. 'Burying something under the bed of a man who, even according to Doctor Mincing, seems to be gripped by some kind of demonic force . . .'

'We're going to find out more.' Harry kept watching the rickety boathouse, but no sign of the men could be seen. 'Not now, it's still too light; there's too much chance of being seen, even for me. But later, once it gets properly dark, we'll come back and go inside and—'

'*Billie! Billie!*'

Voices, faint and high, floated through the rain. Harry swung around and saw a shape moving towards them over the water. He watched it, waiting for it to become clear.

It was a boat the same size as theirs. In it were two small children, digging the water with their paddles. Harry recognized them from the jetty the previous day, when they had been some of the first to run forward and greet Billie. They were waving at her now, their faces wild with fear.

'Fire! Fire at Fisherman's Point!'

# Chapter Nine

Billie leapt out of the boat even as it glided up to the jetty. Harry tied up the ropes, jumped out with Arthur, and ran after her. Everywhere he saw the Islanders shouting, waving their arms. He ran on, following Billie towards the smoking remains of one of the huts.

It was one of the smaller ones, out on the edge of the village. Its roof had collapsed and smoke still billowed from it, thick and black. Some of the Islanders were throwing buckets of water onto the wreckage, and Billie ran to help them, only to stop and turn towards Auntie May, who was running towards her, arms outstretched.

'I saw them, Billie! I saw them!'

'Who?' Billie embraced her old friend, even as she glared at the blackened remains of the hut.

'Men from the town! Members of Oscar Dupont's mob.' Auntie May shook her head. 'I was near the jetty when I saw them. They were running down it and then leapt into their boat. Taunted me, they did, and waved one of their placards too. I thought they were blustering at first, just trying to frighten us—but then I saw the smoke! Their work was done.'

'Anyone hurt?' Harry grabbed a bucket and hurled water onto the smoking ruins.

'No, thank heaven! And the hut can be rebuilt— although I fear there may be little to gain from that.' Auntie May pointed back towards the river, and the city across it. 'They will be back, I am sure. The more Dupont's mob rages, the braver they become! They will be back, and in greater numbers.' She gestured to everyone nearby. 'That is what we must prepare for, as best we can. Follow me, my fellow Islanders! To Brother Jacques' hut! He will do for us what he can. Billie, you and your friends must come too. Follow!'

She hurried off, and the Islanders did as she asked, following her towards a dark looming shape nearby, the large hut that Harry recognized as the one he had visited the day before. He heard chanting coming from it, the sound of hundreds of voices, and then he noticed a familiar figure standing by it too, just by the doorway.

'A calamity! *Une catastrophe!*'

It was Madame Melrose. She was shaking her head and walking forward to comfort Auntie May. Harry saw that the elegantly dressed lady's face was flushed and that, like the Islanders, she too was holding a bucket of water and dousing the flames. Her voice was broken and distressed.

'I know, Auntie May! I saw them too, as they fled from their vile act. How can it be? I come to help you, as acting head of the council—but I have no sooner arrived than I find myself standing powerless while you deal with this outrage. Unbearable!'

'You must not blame yourself, Madame.' Auntie May placed an arm on the lady's sleeve.

'But I do. I do—why, *mes enfants*. We meet again.' Madame Melrose had noticed Harry and his friends drawing near. She peered at them. 'What brings you to Fisherman's Point at this terrible time? Do you not have to set off for Tobermory Swamp?'

'One of us has friends living here.' Harry gestured at Billie. *No need to lie; the truth can do just as well.* 'Thought we'd stop here and say hello before going back.'

'Friends with the Islanders?' Madame Melrose wiped away a tear. 'You choose your friends most wisely. These are fine people—Mayor Monticelso was not the only one to think so. I too have taken a great interest in them, have I not, Auntie May?'

'Yes indeed! A great help to us, over the years! Now if you'll excuse me, ma'am—' Auntie May curtsied, and headed towards the hut's doorway.

'Yes, of course.' Madame Melrose curtsied back, and turned to the children. 'I believe I told you that I was coming for a meeting here? And I did not come alone. For all its hopelessness, no one can say I have not done what I can to help these noble citizens. Come, let me introduce you to these gentlemen here . . .'

Clutching her bucket of water, she set off towards the burnt hut. Harry saw that a small group of men had gathered there, dressed in coats and top hats. Several of them had grabbed buckets too, and were pouring water on the ruins, rain dripping from them as they worked. Madame Melrose walked up to them and emptied her own bucket onto the smoking timbers.

'I asked these gentlemen to come down here several days ago, as soon as this business broke.' Madame Melrose continued. 'They are *professeurs d'anthropologie sociale*, that is to say, professors of social anthropology, the study of human culture. From the University of Chicago. My plan was to use their expert opinions to construct a defence of the Islanders—a clear explanation of why their practices are in no way deserving of these accusations.'

She gestured at the men, who nodded at Harry and his friends. Some carried on dousing the fire, others were writing in notebooks as they stared around the Islanders' huts. All had grim expressions, and Madame Melrose's face was troubled too.

'Terrible, that such a plan is even necessary. The Islanders are strong, intelligent people, and are perfectly capable of making a defence themselves, but no one, in these terrible times, will listen to them, will they? Indeed, I wonder if anyone will even listen to my anthropological friends. The mob do more than make accusations now, *mes professeurs*! Attacks on the Islanders' homes indeed! Where will it end?'

'An unfortunate business, ma'am.' One of the gentlemen tipped his hat; the others shook their heads.

'I am powerless. I see the criminals flee in their boat and can do nothing. That Oscar Dupont and his inflammatory speeches—I can do nothing about him either. What hope do we have of stopping this fury, the anthropologists and I?' She turned towards the main hut, from which the chanting could still be heard. 'They are at their rituals, the Islanders. I fear that may be the hope that remains for them . . . But I shall continue to do what I can. Come gentlemen, we must fetch more water . . .'

She hurried off with her bucket, and the top-hatted

gentlemen followed. Harry watched them go, Madame Melrose stopping to comfort Islanders as they passed. The anthropologists were doing the same. Harry felt Billie tug at his hand.

'Come on.' She started walking towards the main hut. The chanting kept drifting. 'Madame Melrose is right—they're doing one of their rituals. We should see it. Might even be useful to take part.'

'How do you mean?' Arthur looked at her curiously.

'They let me take part before, when I lived with them.' Billie shrugged. 'Said it would protect me. I can't be sure, but I reckon it might have. That journey all the way up to New York, all those scrapes I managed to get out of—do you really think I could have pulled that off on my own?'

'That's what you've always told us,' said Harry.

'Who knows?' Billie shrugged again. 'It won't do us any harm, that's for sure. Might even do a bit of good.' She looked back at the blackened remains, and shook her head. 'And I'd say we need all the help we can get, wouldn't you?'

They ducked through the doorway. It took Harry's eyes even longer to adjust to the darkness this time, because only the murkiest light filtered through the hut's windows, and that was blocked by the bodies gathered inside. Harry made out new odours, of burning oil, herbs. He saw that Billie and Arthur had sat down amongst the Islanders, and he sat down too, just by the door. Brother Jacques sat at the centre of the hut, staring straight at him.

'You have come amongst us again, I see—you are no longer so suspicious of our ways.' The old man lowered his face, and it disappeared into shadow. 'Indeed, I hear from Auntie May that you, Billie, and Arthur seek to help us Islanders, to investigate this business, to clear our name. If so, then it is right you all join us now. You will have need of our spirits' magic. Great need, I believe.'

There was a scraping sound. Harry looked down to see Brother Jacques opening one of the engraved brass jars, his voice softer, just a whisper.

'There is great evil abroad in New Orleans—no one can deny it. And so we call upon the spirits to help us, to protect us. Let us hope that they protect you too, as you delve into these dark matters . . .'

'Let us hope,' said Auntie May, leaning out of the shadows. Her eyes shone, and Harry saw a small brass amulet swinging by a chain from her hand, on which birds' wings and snakes were engraved.

'The spirit of the earth.' Brother Jacques reached into the jar. 'Let it move among us.'

Auntie May held up a brand from the fire, and the

rim of the jar danced with light. Brother Jacques lifted out the dried snakeskin, the coiled-up shape rotating in his grip. Auntie May leant the brand closer, its flames just brushing the snakeskin. Only the very edge of it started to burn, but thick plumes of smoke spiralled. Harry blinked, and saw Billie and Arthur were blinking too, as Brother Jacques reached into the jar a second time.

'The spirit of the sky,' he said. 'It descends, and is with us.'

He took out the hawk feathers. The flames brushed them, and more smoke spilled in the darkness, mingling with the smoke from the skin. Harry's eyes stung harder, and his vision blurred, but he carried on looking as Brother Jacques reached into the jar again.

'The spirit of the trees,' he said. 'It grows within us.'

He held up the branches. He took just one of the dried pods and tossed it into the flames, which shot up and turned bright green. *Interesting*, thought Harry, as the smoke swept up around him, thick and swirling. *An impossible amount, for such a small seed.* The plumes sprawled in different directions, and whatever had been making his eyes sting was far more powerful now, because the pain had become quite intense, and he could see nothing at all. But he could hear, and he sat in the swirling gloom, listening to the Islanders' chanting.

'The spirits will protect us . . . The spirits will protect us . . .'

*Maybe,* thought Harry. *But me, Artie, and Billie need to help too—and the sooner the better.*

Silently he gathered his legs underneath him. The hut's door was just a few feet away, and his hand groped through the door, and found its frame. He pulled himself up and stepped out into the fine rain that was still falling from the murky grey sky. He waited, blinking, while the stinging faded from his eyes, and his vision returned. Then he walked away from the hut, smoke curling from his clothes, the Islanders' chanting growing fainter. But something Brother Jacques had said lingered in his thoughts:

*There is great evil abroad in New Orleans.*

He walked past the remains of the hut, and down to the end of the jetty. He stood there as the rain fell from the swollen clouds. He made out the buildings on the other side of the river. He turned, and stared in the direction of where he knew the old boathouse waited, where he knew two men, one with a dagger-like beard, the other with yellowed eyes, would be found. He thought of all he had seen in New Orleans in the short time since he and his friends had arrived.

*The mob, their hate-filled placards thrust into the air.*

*Mayor Monticelso's face, stretched wide with terror.*

*A man searching a room with a hook in his hand, its barbs catching the light . . .*

Once again, he felt his heart quicken. Pulses twitched, and he felt those flickering sensations creeping all over his skin. *Just like before a trick—but I've never felt them quite like this before,* he thought. His heart throbbed almost painfully, and the flickers were more powerful too, like little electrical jolts. He could feel trickles of perspiration making their way down his back, across his chest, down the back of his legs.

*A little nervousness is a good thing,* he told himself. *Use it to focus. Use it to concentrate.*

And his heart kept throbbing, those flickering sensations kept gathering strength, the droplets of sweat kept gliding, as he stood there in the rain, staring at the city, and trying to work out what might lie ahead.

# Chapter Ten

The boat sailed through the darkening water. Billie gripped the rudder and Arthur sat up in the prow, Harry crouched beside him. As the wharfs of the city drew near, Harry could still smell the scented smoke in his friend's clothes.

'It was pretty much as I expected, that ritual,' Arthur was saying. 'I told you, I've read about this vodou business, and about other kinds of magic too. All over the world people use spells and charms to help people, to heal them, and sometimes it really does seem as if they have genuine power—people get better, their troubles vanish. Scientific proof or not.' He lifted the sleeve of his coat and breathed in the scent. 'Anyway, it was good of the Islanders to offer us protection.'

'They're good people.' Billie narrowed her eyes as she guided the boat up to the wharf. 'Here's your stop, Artie.'

'Ah, yes.' Arthur put one hand on the ladder at the wharf's side. 'I have to say, as far as protection goes, you're the ones who are going to need it far more than me. Are you sure you don't want me to come with you? Seems wrong, me heading off to the library, when I think where you're going. Back to that boathouse where—'

'We'll just spy on them. A quick look and we'll be gone.' Billie cut him off. 'And we've just agreed, haven't we? The more we learn about demons and magic the better. If it turns out that the men at the boathouse really *are* working some kind of evil curse on the mayor—well, we'll need to know everything we can.'

'It's the only way we can clear the Islanders—by finding out the truth, every last bit of it.' Harry nodded. 'And no one finds stuff out quicker than you, Artie.'

He exchanged glances with Billie. Neither of them had said anything to each other, but he knew she felt the same about their younger friend taking part in their return to the boathouse. *Anyway, it's true,* he thought. *Artie really is good at finding things out.*

'If you're sure.' Arthur clambered up the ladder and stood on the wharf. Gas lamps stood all along its length, making the misty rain glow. 'I've got permission to enter the library after opening hours; it's part of my special membership. I'll start off in the Magic and Folklore section—that'll have lots about curses and demons and the like.'

'That's the idea, Artie.' Billie pushed the boat off. 'We'll meet you there in a couple of hours.'

'I'll have gone through half the section by then.' Arthur took out his notebook and pen, and waved them at his friends. 'I'm already familiar with the cataloguing system, remember?'

Arthur headed up the wharf while Harry grabbed hold of an oar and stirred the water, swinging the boat round. Rope whispered, the sail billowed and Billie pushed out the rudder, her gaze fixed ahead. Harry glanced back at Arthur, quite a small shape in the distance already, clambering up the steps at the end of the wharf.

The boat caught the current. The next time Harry looked back, Arthur was gone, and so was the wharf. He concentrated on helping Billie, following her instructions as she guided the boat on. Then he sat back and held up his hand and watched the water gather on it, carefully trying to keep it so still that the droplets didn't move at all. He glanced back at Billie, who was sitting in the stern, one hand clutching a rope, the other the boat's rudder. Both her hands, he noticed, were trembling slightly.

Ten minutes later they saw the boathouse, a dark shape in the rain.

'You can just drop me off, if you like,' Harry whispered. 'Wait for me out here on the river. Might be easier if I went alone.'

'Alone?' Billie's hands tightened their grip. 'I don't think so, Harry. Who's going to help you out if something goes wrong, eh?'

'I'm just saying—'

'This is the Islanders we're talking about. They're my friends.' Billie pushed out the rudder. 'Come on.'

The boat curved up to the shore; the prow buried itself silently in the mud. Harry and Billie leapt out and ran along the beach to the rickety steps leading up to the boathouse. Harry stared up at the old, broken-down building, and saw that the windows were dark.

'No one's in there,' he whispered. 'Let's go in. Maybe there'll be something inside that'll tell us who they are, or what they're doing—'

Harry stopped. He grabbed Billie's arm and pulled her back behind the steps. He had seen something further down the beach—several tiny points of red light. Crouched in the shadows, he watched them brighten and fade, and brighten again. *Tobacco pipes.* Keeping a hand on Billie's arm, he pulled her after him, dodging between the boats that lay along the water's edge, breathing in odours of fish and tar. One boat was turned over and they hid behind it, peering around its stern. Harry breathed in the stench of tobacco as he made out the small group of figures gathered around another turned-over boat.

'It's them, Billie. Right ahead,' Harry whispered.

Daggerbeard and Yelloweyes stood nearest, sucking on their pipes, with bottles in their fists. Yelloweyes was almost motionless, but Daggerbeard stared about in the gloom. Other men, about five of them, were gathered round, and Harry saw two more hurrying out of the mist. Harry edged forward, trying to hear scraps of conversation, but then Daggerbeard's stare turned in his direction, and he pushed himself back, angling his arms and legs so that they fitted into the darkest shadows, his teeth biting into his lip.

*The hook, glinting in the light.* Harry remembered it, and Daggerbeard's stare as he struggled in the dumb waiter shaft. But he heard the mutterings of conversation continue, and he peered back round the stern to see that Daggerbeard was looking away again, concentrating on his pipe.

'Come on,' he whispered to Billie.

They dodged back along the beach, keeping to the shadows. Reaching the boathouse steps, Harry looked back at the glowing pipes again, making sure they hadn't moved, before leading Billie up the steps. Together, they reached the door at the top. Harry tested the handle, found it was unlocked, and pushed the door open, pulling Billie in after him.

It was dark inside but Harry's eyes quickly adjusted to the gloom. He edged forward. Nets hung on the walls and he made out spears and jagged harpoons dangling from the rafters, their edges glinting. The smell of fish guts curled up his nose.

'I was right. Definitely fishermen,' Billie muttered.

Harry nodded, and edged further into the room. He noticed a table on the far side with a small, bulging shape on it.

It was the sack.

'Don't touch it.' Billie reached for him, but Harry only felt the tips of her fingers brush his shoulder, because he was already moving forward. 'Maybe it's a trap, leaving it out like that,' she hissed.

'Maybe.' Harry crouched over it.

'Even if it isn't—careful.' Billie grabbed his shoulder properly. 'If it's something to do with what happened to Mayor Monticelso . . . Remember what a state he's in. Taken over by a demonic force!'

'How else are we going to find out what's going on?'

Harry couldn't help noticing that he was trembling

a little. He steadied his hand, moving it smoothly to the sack's neck. His finger and thumb took hold of the cloth and pulled it. He heard Billie's breathing, just next to his ear. The sack was slightly open and he peered in, but could see only darkness. He pulled again, and then stumbled back as the sack fell open, its contents spilling onto the table.

Billie had stopped breathing. Harry realized that he wasn't breathing either, and he forced himself to suck in air. He leant forward, inspecting what lay there.

A bushel of dried branches, crowded with blackened seeds. Three withered, coiled-up snakeskins. Five hawks' feathers, tied with a cord.

'That's impossible,' Billie spluttered. 'The Islanders . . . That's what they use for their magic . . . Their good magic . . . We saw them use it just now.'

'I don't understand.'

Harry reached forward and touched the feathers. His fingers moved across, brushing against the seeds, the snakeskins, and back to the feathers again. *Work it out.* He closed his eyes, saw the objects hanging in the darkness, and moved them about in his mind, as if they were the pieces of some kind of puzzle . . .

'Harry!'

His eyes flicked open. Billie was staring at him in alarm. He heard the voices and the tread of boots up the steps. He saw the handle of the boathouse door, turning.

Harry grabbed the sack and scooped the objects back into it, positioning it on the table just where it had been. He whirled round, checking for another way out, but there wasn't time.

The door was already opening, and boots thudded, voices muttered, as Daggerbeard and Yelloweyes led the men in.

# Chapter Eleven

The nets stank of fish. River water dripped from them as they hung on the boathouse wall and Harry, hidden behind them, flinched as a trickle snaked down his face. He felt Billie flinch too and grabbed her arm, steadying her. Even that slight move, he noticed, made the nets sway, their wetness catching the light. He peered out through the foul-smelling strands and listened to the fishermen.

'We're all here then.'

'Six o'clock, just like you said.'

'Tell us what's going on. Tell us quick . . .'

There were about twenty of them, tugging wooden stools into a circle. They sat down, delving into tobacco pouches and drinking from their bottles. A couple of men crouched over an iron brazier, and soon flames crept up from it, throwing light around the circle of faces, every one of them staring towards Daggerbeard and Yelloweyes, who were sitting by an upturned boat hull. The faces were suspicious, and Harry heard mutterings, snarls. But they fell silent as Daggerbeard rose and walked towards the sack on the table.

The brazier's flames brightened as he lurched past. Shadows of his bulk slanted around the boathouse. He reached for the sack and emptied it—feathers, snakeskins, and seeds spilled onto the table. Daggerbeard pointed at the items.

'The demon curse. Don't you worry, it'll do for its victims.' His voice growled through a thin smile. '*The Islanders,* I mean.'

Harry narrowed his eyes and he saw Billie doing the same. His hand tightened on her arm. The fishermen were still motionless, but Daggerbeard's shadows hurtled around the room as he strode round the circle.

'We'll free this town of them! Every last one of them!' Daggerbeard growled.

'About time! Filthy folk with their dangerous ways!' Yelloweyes glared at the sack's contents. 'Who knows if that stuff of theirs summons demons or not? But once we've done the job, once we've tucked it under the floorboards just where Monticelso's sleeping, once we've sent a little note to the New Orleans police telling them where to look, that little sack'll whisk up demons of one kind, just you see!'

'There'll be rioting in the streets! The Islanders'll be forced to run. No one'll have a doubt they're behind the demon curse and they'll be gone. And we know what happens then, don't we?' Daggerbeard swung round. 'It'll be ours! Fisherman's Point!'

*Fisherman's Point.* The words echoed around the boathouse. Harry listened to every lingering trace of them and, with each echo, the business became clearer to him. *So that's what's going on—these men want the Islanders' land . . .* Huddled behind the net he watched the fishermen, who had scowls on their faces, and were snarling at Daggerbeard and his friend.

'That's all very well—but when, eh?'

'Three days ago you asked for our money. What's happened since?'

'Nothing, that's what! You tried this plan of yours, and you failed!'

'Now you're asking for more cash—'

'Sure we are!' Daggerbeard bellowed. 'It's turned out more difficult than we thought, every bit of it! Right from the very start—pickpocketing the keys from one of the city hall servants. Any of you quick enough to do that? First we had to find out where they hung out and smoked their pipes, near that alleyway. Then there was the snatching itself . . .' From his jacket he took out a length of fishing line, a tiny hook dangling from it. His burly hand performed a complicated move, flicking the hook away and reeling it back in again. 'Used my fisherman's skills. Walked past him, dropped the hook into his pocket, and the keys just flew into my hand.'

'But that's not all we got! Information too— we eavesdropped on them, hiding in the alleyway,' Yelloweyes added. 'That's how we learnt when the mayor would be taken out of his bedroom for his treatment, leaving us time to do the work. Clever, eh? And then there's the charms, getting hold of the charms. The Islanders weren't going to just hand us some, were they?' Yelloweyes jabbed a finger at the items on the table, then reached into his pocket and drew out a leather-bound book. 'Mayor Monticelso's own book, all about those filthy Islanders and their ways. All about their magic too! Wouldn't have been any good to you though—most of you can't even read.'

'And you wouldn't have had the guts for what we did next either: going round pretty much every apothecary and Chinese medicine shop in town, shaking them down, searching for the exact items we needed.' Daggerbeard snatched up a snakeskin. 'Particular skins, particular feathers, particular seeds—we've got pretty much the exact stuff. And who's to say, brought all together, that this junk doesn't *have* some kind of magical power? Brave enough to lay your hands on it, are you? It didn't have nothing to do with Mayor Monticelso, but who knows what else it can do?'

He thrust the snakeskin at the fishermen, who scrambled back with their stools. They were reeling and Harry felt like reeling too, even though his back was firmly against the wall. *Mayor Monticelso's book, detailing the Islanders' rituals. Robbing apothecary and medicine shops all round New Orleans.* The new pieces of information danced in his head, and he felt his face grow hot against the stinking net as he remembered the words that had raced from his lips earlier that day. *Of course they're behind it . . .* He thought of how certain he had been that the two men, with their mysterious sack, were responsible for the mayor's terrible state.

*They're nothing to do with it. They're just using the situation for their own grubby ends.*

'Twenty years we've been waiting for this moment.' Daggerbeard tossed the snakeskin at Yelloweyes, who caught it, and dropped it back onto the table. 'Us here, we've always felt the same about the Islanders, and maybe others have too. But not pretty much all of New Orleans, like it is now.'

'That Oscar Dupont, he's doing a fine job.' Yelloweyes shuffled from the table, brushing his hands on his coat. 'Whipped up an angry crowd . . .'

'It'll be even angrier soon,' Daggerbeard continued. 'They just need leading on. A bait, something to catch their eye.' He jerked a thumb back towards the snakeskin, feathers and seeds. 'And that's what we've got. Just need to put it where we need it, that's all.'

'We'll go back! We know the way in now—it'll be even easier!' Yelloweyes was taking his turn to circle. 'Who can blame us for deciding to go back later, when we were disturbed? If we'd been caught, we two might have been the ones to get the blame for the demon curse then, not the Islanders—any of you thought of that? But we'll finish the job, don't you worry! We'll plant it all under the floorboards, like we said.'

'It'll sit there, an undiscovered clue.' Daggerbeard grinned. 'But it'll be discovered soon enough. Maybe the police will get that little note, or maybe it'll be Oscar Dupont—haven't decided yet.' His grin widened. 'One way or another, our little sack of stuff will see the light again and then . . .'

'Fisherman's Point will be ours.' Yelloweyes slapped a fist into a palm. 'As for Mayor Monticelso, gripped by a demon curse—who knows who's responsible for that . . . and who cares!'

Harry's face grew even hotter. The damp strands, warmed by his blushing skin, released their stench even more freely. *Wrong, so wrong.* He stared through the net at the items on the table. *Exactly the same as the ones in the ritual*, he thought—the fishermen had worked with care. *Unlike me.* He remembered looking down at that table just a few minutes before, startled and amazed, trying to move the bits and pieces about in his mind: sluggish, slow, fumbling. *So wrong . . .*

'Fisherman's Point—the best bit of fisherman's land in New Orleans, or anywhere near it!' Daggerbeard bellowed at the fishermen.

'We've always deserved that land. Since always!' Yelloweyes snapped. 'Not right that they have it! Decent land deserves decent folk living on it! Perfect for building jetties, as we all know! Catches the currents leading down to the sea, too . . .'

'And the best thing about our plan is, there's no one'll want it after the Islanders have gone.' Daggerbeard gathered up the items on the table, scooping them back into the sack. 'Who's going to set foot on it, with all the rumours of evil magic?'

'We'll buy it off the city for next to nothing.' Yelloweyes chuckled. 'Any of us with a few dollars to spare, we'll be able to grab Fisherman's Point, hut by hut.'

'We'll double our jetties! Our gutting houses and boat-building huts too!' Daggerbeard fumbled after one of the snakeskins, which was rolling away.

'Let the Islanders tie their boats to whatever far-off bit of the Mississippi they get driven to,' Yelloweyes continued. 'And if they get driven back to the island they came from, all that time ago—why, then they can tie their boats up there too.'

'The demon curse. It'll work like . . .' Daggerbeard laughed. 'Like magic.'

He scooped the last few items into the sack. But he fumbled again, and one of the hawk's feathers fluttered off the table, catching a warm current of air from the brazier. Daggerbeard snatched at it but it spiralled upwards, and looped the loop. Harry saw it and flinched, tightening his grip on Billie's arm.

It was heading straight for them. It had left behind the current of air but it was still journeying on, circling, looping. Daggerbeard was watching it, his eyes following its path, as if those curls and loops reminded him of the cleverness of his plan.

The hawk's feather landed on the netting. It nestled in the strands, just in front of Harry's face, and Daggerbeard wasn't staring at the feather anymore.

He was staring at them.

# Chapter Twelve

'Don't let them get away!'

The fishermen's fists plunged into the nets. Harry tried to break free, but the criss-crossing strings drew tight, snaring his hands and feet. Burly arms worked quickly, hoisting the nets into the air, and Harry was upside-down, his body tangled with Billie's. Harry saw the spears and harpoons hanging from the rafters, the brazier's light dancing on their edges. He struggled harder, and then felt himself fall. He and Billie, still tangled in the nets, thudded onto the floor in front of Daggerbeard's boots.

'Who are they?!' Daggerbeard spluttered.

There was a hook in his hand; Harry recognized it, the exact pattern of its jagged tip. It hovered over him as Yelloweyes pulled expertly at the net, making the criss-cross strands slide away. Harry and Billie sprawled on the floor, and the fishermen gathered round, looking down at their catch.

'Get off us! Let us go!' Billie cried.

A burly fist pushed her back down, and the hook hovered closer. Harry's heart pounded. His eyes fixed on the brazier. It was burning quite fiercely, its flames leaping over its edge. *Think of something.* He looked back at the fishermen. In amongst them, Yelloweyes jabbed a finger down at Billie.

'Who cares who they are—spies, that's *what* they are, and that's all that matters.' Spit flew. 'If they've heard . . . So much for our plan . . .'

'Good riddance to it! Fisherman's Point belongs to the Islanders, you remember that!' Billie lurched up again but thudded back onto the floor.

'Steady now,' Daggerbeard muttered at Yelloweyes. His fist stayed gripped around the hook. 'They're kids.'

'And?'

'So no one's going to believe them, are they?'

'What makes you so sure? Maybe they will, maybe they won't!' Yelloweyes' nose wrinkled. 'This girl, what's she doing speaking out for the Islanders? Maybe she knows 'em—maybe she'll go and tell 'em too. Then the filthy folk'll be ready for what we spring on them, able to explain it away and . . .'

'Don't you talk about them like that! Don't you dare—'

A heavy hand slammed over her mouth, choking off the words. Harry felt the fishermen's hands grip him too, but he realized his left foot was free. Just a few inches away stood the table with the sack on it. *The sack, into which Daggerbeard had stuffed the snakeskins, the seeds, and all but one of the feathers.* It lay there, its neck half-tied, its contents safe. *The same contents that produced, even just a few of them, that smoke.* Harry studied the sack and then checked the brazier again, several yards away across the boathouse, its flames waiting. His boot swivelled, practising a move, and he slid it slowly across, hooking its toe around one of the wooden legs.

'Maybe best to be safe.' Daggerbeard turned away with Yelloweyes.

'It'll be easy enough.' Yelloweyes lowered his voice. 'Already caught them in our nets, like fish out of the sea. We'll just wrap them back up, take them out on our boat. Throw the nets down into the water, like we always do. Who's to say what's tangled up in them . . .'

'Billie! The spirits!' The words, tiny noises, hissed out of the corner of Harry's mouth. 'The Islanders' spirits, remember?!'

A fisherman's hand was covering Billie's face, but Harry could see her eyes. They flickered a few times, and then they squeezed so tightly shut that almost every other bit of her face clenched with the effort.

*She's understood.* Harry checked the distance between the sack on the table and the brazier again, and adjusted his boot so that it gripped the table leg even more securely. His eyes slanted to the door and he saw, propped next to it, an old rowing paddle. *The last bit of the trick.*

'Sure, we'll lose some good netting.' Yelloweyes was still muttering. 'But that won't be hard to replace and—'

Harry tipped the table over. The sack slid off it, but Harry's boot flew up in time and kicked it at the exact angle he needed. The sack spun, arched through the air and shot straight down towards the brazier, glancing against the steel rim and tumbling into the flames, which shot up, a furious green. Plumes of smoke sprawled, just like in Brother Jacques' hut but twenty times thicker, and Harry kept his gaze fixed on Billie. Her eyes were still shut, like two screwed-up fists, and he knew the plan would work, as he squeezed his own eyes shut too.

'I can't see!'

'What have they done?!'

'Don't let them get away!'

'My eyes! My eyes!'

The fishermen's fists fell away. The wooden floor shuddered as boots stumbled, bodies thudded to the ground. Every one of the fishermen, Harry knew, would be digging into their eyes, trying to rid them of that stinging blur and he felt a faint stinging in his own eyes too, as a few wisps found their way through the squeezed lids. He rolled over, boots thundering, hands scrabbling around him, and he kept his face as close as he could to the ground. Only then did he risk a blink.

'This way, Billie! Follow me!'

The smoke was thinner down by the ground. He saw scrambling boots, collapsing bodies and, beyond them, the boathouse door. He spotted Billie's hand and grabbed it. His eyes squeezed shut again but that image, of the boathouse door, hovered on. He scrabbled forward, tugging Billie after him, and reached the door. He grabbed the paddle hanging from the hook behind it for the last part of the trick, just in time.

'The door! Get to the door, everyone! That's how they'll escape!' one of the fishermen yelled.

Harry held the paddle like a spear and flung it as hard as he could across the boathouse, aiming it so it would fly over the fishermen's heads. He heard a crash, and the shattering of a window. The whole boathouse shuddered as every fisherman spun around in the direction of the sound.

'They're trying to get out the back!'

'Stop them!'

*Just like a trick.* Harry pulled Billie out onto the steps. *All a matter of making your audience look in the wrong place*—and there was nowhere more pointless to look right now than on the other side of the boathouse. He stumbled down the stairs. His eyes were open and he felt a little blurriness, a mild stinging, but that was all. He leapt onto the soft mud of the beach, Billie landing beside him. They reached their boat and, with a shove of his shoulder, Harry launched it.

'Maybe you were right about the Islanders' magic, Billie,' Harry said, as they scrambled into the boat.

'What?'

'About it protecting you. Looks like it got you out of another sticky situation just now. Me too . . .' He couldn't help a tiny smile from forming on his face as he dug the water with an oar. 'Not a bad stunt, that.'

'ROW, HARRY! ROW!'

They were out on the river, but Billie was pointing back at the boathouse. At the top of the steps the fishermen were stumbling out through the door, their boots slithering in the wet sand, their fists still rubbing their eyes. Harry made out the voices of Daggerbeard and Yelloweyes, thundering through the rain.

'Stop them!'

*Too late.* Harry tugged on the oars, Billie pulled up the sail, and the boat glided away. Back on the shore the fishermen were toppling down the steps onto the beach, and a few of them even managed to reach their boats, fumbling, cursing. A couple of skiffs bobbed away from the shore, but the occupants floundered, unable to see. Harry stopped rowing because the sail had caught the wind; the boat shot through the water, leaving the fishermen behind. Billie sat in the stern, looking back at the struggling shapes still visible on the shore. Rain trickled down her cheeks; her eyes blazed.

'Don't worry, at least we managed to wreck their plan.' Harry slotted the oars into their holders. 'If they go back, if they try and put anything under the mayor's bed, we'll tell everyone about it—the Islanders will never get the blame. Anyway, they haven't even got the stuff anymore; it's all gone up in smoke and—'

'It doesn't make any difference, does it?' Billie's head snapped round. Her eyes were glaring at him now, not the men on the shore. 'Can't you see that? CAN'T YOU?'

The boat flew on. The rain fell even more thickly, coating Harry's face, but he felt it burn away almost immediately. The blush was back, even more powerful than before, and he felt blood throb in his cheeks, his jaw, even down his neck. He looked up at Billie and saw tears spilling from her eyes.

'Sorry, Harry. It's not your fault. It's just . . .' Her head sunk onto her chest. 'So maybe we've managed to stop their plan. But the only reason it would have ever worked in the first place was because this whole city's rising up against the Islanders, isn't it? And we haven't done anything about that, have we?'

'I . . . I guess not . . .'

'You saw Oscar Dupont! You saw the crowd—they burned down one of the Islanders' huts, didn't they? Who knows what they'll do next! If they don't discover something under a floor, do you think it'll be long before they find another excuse?' She grabbed a rope. 'As far as New Orleans is concerned, this demon curse is still on the loose. So it doesn't matter what we found out, back there. The demon curse—until we discover the truth behind it, the Islanders are in as much danger as ever.'

'I know—'

The wind snatched the words from Harry's mouth. He tried to think of other ones, of anything to say at all, but his lips remained still. Crouched in the boat, he ran back over everything that had happened ever since the moment when those two burly figures had appeared in Mayor Monticelso's office. He thought of how carefully he had followed the two men, how determinedly he had broken into the boathouse to spy on them, how certain he had been. *Wrong, wrong about everything* . . .

'Come on.' Billie's voice was softer now. 'Maybe Artie's discovered something. He said he'd have got through half of Magic and Folklore by now, remember?'

The rain drove harder against the sail, making the boat fly on. Clouds of mist swirled in the darkness. Billie frowned, but she seemed to be concentrating on the ropes of the boat, tugging at them so that the boat curved towards the city and its wharfs. Harry joined in, undoing knots. *Maybe she's right; maybe Arthur will have found something.*

The boat sailed up to a wharf. Billie tied it to a post, and Harry followed her along the wharf's planks. Together, they made their way through the rainy streets. The iron balconies dripped and, up in the sky, the dark clouds glimmered around their edges. Thunder echoed all around. Harry and Billie reached the main square and hurried over to the New Orleans Public Library, where a crowd had gathered outside.

Harry stopped. It was Oscar Dupont's mob. He recognized the placards, and some of the faces too, even more fearful and hateful than the last time. People were joining the crowd all the time, pouring out of the surrounding streets. Some carried banners; some were carrying poles with lanterns dangling from them, each one bright with flames. In the middle of it all was Oscar Dupont, rain spattering off his bald head, his eyes gleaming, his arms jabbing as he addressed the crowd. *More hateful words*, thought Harry, but then he found himself listening to those words quite carefully, taking in each one.

'The demon curse! It has struck again!'

'What's that?' Billie was frozen beside Harry too. 'What—'

'Follow me,' said Harry, urgently.

He didn't quite recognize his own voice. It hung there in the rain, unusually high, as he threw himself into the crowd. His body felt unfamiliar and awkward too, his legs weak, his arms slow. He tried to push through the crowd, and pushed again, but remained where he was, and he wondered whether it would be possible to make his way to the front. But then the crowd broke apart in front of him, a corridor forming all the way up to the library's doors.

'Let them through!'

'They're his friends, aren't they?'

'Orphans from a swamp school! They came to City Hall this morning!'

'Let them through!'

Harry ran. His legs trembled but they kept moving under him, and he arrived at the library doors. Billie blundered into his back, and he saw that her face was pale, her mouth open. Together they ran into the hall and saw a group of men up at the top of the library's main staircase. They raced up the stairs, pushed past the men, and stumbled into a domed reading room.

Harry saw him.

He reached out and grabbed the corner of a desk, taking in the piles of books, the scattered papers.

And he saw the boy's body, slightly smaller than his own, spread out on the floor, his back arched, limbs shaking.

Arthur.

# Chapter Thirteen

'Found right there!' one of the men shouted.

'Stretched out and trembling!'

'The curse! The curse!'

'The demon has entered him!'

Pain shot through Harry's knees as he slammed down onto the polished floor. He crouched over Arthur, staring at his face. He hardly recognized it. His friend's familiar features, that gentle mouth, those enquiring eyes, were a tangled wreck. Harry felt the floor shudder and saw the back of Arthur's head jolting against it. He tried to hold it still.

'A poor orphan boy!' A frail voice cut through the crowd. 'Why, he and his friends visited Mayor Monticelso earlier today! To comfort him, to aid his recovery. To think that one of them should end up suffering the same fate!'

Doctor Mincing toppled in. The feeble-bodied

doctor was in a completely distressed state, his hair flying in all directions, his hands fumbling with a stethoscope. Those dark-ringed eyes stared at the sprawling figure, and then at Harry.

'Forgive me!' A feeble croak fell from his lips. 'If only I could offer you the slightest help. But what I told you this morning remains true now—I know nothing of this condition! Despite my years of study, my field trips, my journey into the jungles of Costa Rica . . .' He lowered his head. 'It is just as it was with our poor mayor. The shaking will only increase from now. Soon, I shall have to arrange for your poor friend to be pinioned. For his own protection, you understand . . .'

'Just tell us what happened! Tell us—'

The floor shook harder. Billie's knees had thudded onto it too, and she crouched over Arthur. Tears flooded from her eyes as she tried to say more, but her voice was a dry gasp, impossible to hear. Doctor Mincing hesitated, then continued.

'I was attending to Mayor Monticelso at City Hall,' he spluttered. 'A distressing enough business, but then a messenger burst in with news of a further terrible incident at the public library. I came directly. My medical knowledge, faced with these awful incidents, seems more useless by the hour, and yet I must do what I can!' He bent unsteadily over Arthur, as if to examine him. 'What can I say—is there any history of nervous disease in your friend's family, perhaps? Anything that might explain his sudden collapse? Had he exhibited any unusual patterns of behaviour in the last few hours perhaps . . .'

'Nothing.' Harry's throat felt choked and swollen. 'He was just helping us.'

'Helping you? In what way?'

'We were trying to find out what happened to Mayor Monticelso . . .' Billie managed another gasp. 'The three of us, we wanted to—'

'Arthur came here to do research.' Harry spotted his friend's notebook, fallen by his body. His hand shook, but he picked it up. 'Look, Billie—he was making notes and everything.'

'Notes? Notes about what?' Doctor Mincing stared at the notebook. 'What does it say? Read it! Perhaps some chance jotting might suggest something that happened to him in the minutes before the attack.'

'It's a list of books.' Harry peered at his friend's handwriting, surrounded by inky splatters. '*Magical Charms of the East Indies. Sorcery in Modern Siberia. A History of Supernatural Trances.* All about magic . . .'

'Ah yes, and he does appear to be in the section for books regarding such matters.' Doctor Mincing pointed at the nearby bookshelves, and at a small brass sign hanging nearby. *Magic and Folklore*, it said. 'It would seem your friend, like so many others, was putting Mayor Monticelso's disease down to supernatural causes. Brave fellow, to delve into such matters.'

'And he has paid the price! The price we shall all pay, if we let this menace remain within our city!'

It was Oscar Dupont. He stood in the doorway of the Reading Room, the crowd swelling behind him with their banners and placards. Dupont's eyes flashed as they fixed on the shape on the library floor. One arm swung forward and pointed at Arthur; the other flew up, a fist punching the air. He was almost dancing as he poured out words faster than ever.

'See what the Islanders will do! A boy! A boy dares to probe their darkness, and their vengeance is swift. They have set the demon on him, just as they did with our poor Monticelso. And if they did that to him, so harmless and young, whom will they spare?'

'GET OUT! The Islanders didn't have anything to do with it!'

Billie was marching right up to him. Somehow, she had recovered her voice, and her strength too, and her boots pounded across the floor. Harry saw the tears on her face trail backwards with the speed of her march.

'You? Why, I remember our conversation just this morning.' Dupont smiled. 'You are a friend of the poor victim? How tragic. I remember how gently I tried to put you right this morning. A shame that it has taken a far more brutal event to reveal how little you understand these matters—'

'Leave us in peace, will you?!'

'Again, the Islanders have struck!' Another punch of his fist, and Dupont swung round to address the crowd. 'As I, your one loyal councillor, predicted. Pity this poor, brave boy—he was about to stumble on proof of their evil charms, I'll be bound, but they set the demon upon him! And now we must take action of our own! We must rid this town of these villains and—'

'GET OUT! GET OUT!' Billie yelled.

She slammed the doors on him and fumbled with the key in the lock, her hands shaking. Billie turned and tried to head back across the room, but Harry saw that the last remains of her strength had vanished, her legs sinking beneath her. Only Doctor Mincing, grabbing her arm, stopped her collapsing completely. He lowered her beside Arthur on the floor, as carefully as he could.

'Talk to your poor friend, my girl!' The doctor pointed sadly at Arthur. 'I have summoned men to take him to the hospital, but in the meantime, help him cling on to his sanity, to his sense of himself! Gather round him, show your faces! It had no effect on Mayor Monticelso, of course—but you hardly knew him, whereas your relationship with your friend is more powerful. Some memory of normal happiness might help shift this dreadful affliction.'

'It's all my fault, Harry!' Billie could hardly look at Arthur. 'I was the one who wanted to help the Islanders—'

'We all did.' Harry cut her off. 'We all wanted to help—Artie too. That's why he came here to the library; I thought it would be safe but—'

'Nothing's safe around here,' Billie cried. 'Nothing at all.'

Harry stared down at Arthur's face. It was even less recognizable now, the shuddering more violent, those glimpses of his true self even more fleeting, and Harry winced as he took in his friend's eyes, two rippling pools of fear. He leant his ear close to Arthur's lips, those lips that were always saying such fascinating things. He tried to hear if they were saying anything at all now. Fragments, choking sounds, the gritting of teeth. Harry flinched. Arthur's arms and legs were beginning to thrash. *I shall have to arrange for your friend to be pinioned.*

'If it's anyone's fault, Billie, it's mine.' His face was hot again, and his eyes ached with tears. 'I should have worked it all out by now, found out what was going on.'

*Keep going.* He reached forward and tried to examine Arthur's clothes. *Clues, the tiniest trace, the tiniest sign.* But his hands faltered as they searched, fumbling in the pockets, catching themselves in the lining. Giving up, he picked up Arthur's notebook instead, but his hands fumbled again, and the notebook toppled onto the floor. *Impossible.* He saw that Billie wasn't searching at all. She was just tugging at Arthur's body, trying to talk to him as if he were still awake.

'Tell us what happened Artie!' She pounded his chest, and his body shook even harder. 'Tell us!'

'It's too late, I'm afraid,' said a voice.

It wasn't Doctor Mincing. Harry knew that, because the spindly doctor was standing straight in front of him, and hadn't moved his lips at all. A new figure had appeared, down at the far end of the Reading Room. Harry blinked again, and the figure moved towards him at the same time, coming more plainly into view.

A pale suit. A neatly trimmed beard.

It was the man Harry had seen on the train.

It was the man he remembered from New York.

# Chapter Fourteen

Harry's arms hung at his sides, motionless. Billie's hands rested on Arthur's body as it writhed. Her mouth dropped open, and Harry realized that his own mouth was open too, its inside hot and dry. No sound could be heard in the library at all, apart from Arthur's moans, and the creaking of overhead fans.

'Who are you?' At last, Harry managed to speak.

'All in good time.' The man's voice was hard and clear. 'For now, we must concentrate on Arthur, and his extremely dangerous condition—'

'Excuse me, sir!' Doctor Mincing interrupted. 'I, a qualified doctor, am the one attending to these children and their friend and I must insist that—'

'My name is Mr James, and I assure you the organization I represent is better equipped to deal with this matter than you!' The man planted a hand directly on Doctor Mincing's chest. He pushed him, driving him down the aisle. 'It could hardly do worse! You don't seem to have done much to help so far, either with the boy or Mayor Monticelso before him; is that not right, sir? Allow me to speak to these children in private, sir!'

A final push sent Doctor Mincing toppling into a chair. Mr James marched back up the aisle. Reaching Arthur's body, he knelt down next to it, examining it. Harry, still with no idea what to say, took in the neatly trimmed beard, the pale suit. He took in the piercing grey eyes, which were flicking in different directions, carefully inspecting every detail of Arthur's state.

'A mistake, an error of judgement . . .' Mr James frowned. 'This investigation has turned out to be far more sinister than we predicted.'

'Just help us!' Billie cried. 'Whoever you are, help us!'

'Help you? We most certainly will. I have already informed the Order of the White Crow, and help is on its way. But it will not be easy.' The grey eyes were still inspecting Arthur, and they narrowed with concern. 'This demon curse—whatever the explanation behind it—is a truly terrible condition. Had I known, I would never have selected it as your first investigation; I would never have put you on the train to New Orleans.'

'Locked in packing cases! I had to escape!' Harry found his voice.

'You were locked in there for your own safety, and for the security of the investigation—I explained all this quite carefully in the letter.' With a handkerchief, Mr James dabbed away the beads of sweat on Arthur's struggling face. 'I drilled air holes; I left a staple near your hand to assist with your escape—you did read the letter, I trust?'

'Sure we read it—the same letter that, when we first opened it, knocked us out with some kind of chemical dust!' Billie reached into Harry's jacket pocket, and pulled the pale green letter out. 'As for explaining things—I don't think so! All you say is that we're working for the Order of the White Crow . . .' She opened the letter and read. 'Which is devoted to the overthrow of evil and—'

'And has there ever been a more terrible example of evil-doing than this?' Mr James pointed down at Arthur. 'A demon curse, unleashed in New Orleans upon its most senior politician, and now upon a boy, and for who knows what purpose! Evil it most certainly is—evil so hideous that it was clearly, as I say, an error to choose it as the first investigation for you all, no matter how talented you may be.' He clenched a fist around the handkerchief, screwing it into a ball. 'Members of the Order are on their way. You must leave it to us.'

'How can we? Arthur's our friend!' Billie cried.

'Tell us what's going on!' Harry stuffed the letter back in his pocket. 'Even before you drugged us and put us on the train, you were watching us, back in New York. Making notes too. You were planning to do something even then; I saw you!'

'I was researching you. I was gripped by your every move, not to mention the remarkable deeds of your two young friends.' Mr James swung round and stared straight into Harry's eyes. 'Three candidates, I was sure of it. How could I not have selected you all? And the New Orleans case seemed perfect, once my research led me to the useful fact of Billie knowing some of those involved. With her determination to help the Islanders, together with her skills—and the skills of young Arthur here too—I was sure the solution would not remain undetected for long.' He gripped Harry's shoulder. 'But, Harry, you were the candidate who filled me with the greatest confidence of all—and my confidence has only grown. Yesterday you escaped from the suitcase with ease. And then there was the remarkable way you broke into the mayor's office which, I discovered a few hours later, you had achieved by scrambling through the dumb waiter system.' He reached into his coat and pulled out a corked test tube in which, Harry noticed, were some familiar-looking brick crumblings. 'Not to mention the escape you and Billie

143

pulled off just now from the fishermen across the river. I haven't even worked out how you did that yet—'

'Set fire to the Islanders' spirit charms,' Harry said quietly.

'What miraculous skills!' Mr James's face drew closer. 'Skills that dazzled us all at the Order of the White Crow. Skills that make anything seem possible. Such agility! Such quickness of eye and thought! Such immense concentration, when others would simply panic and flail! Most of all, you demonstrate an ability to put these skills into practice not just on the stage, in the world of theatrical magic, but in the real world too, the real world which, as this investigation proves, is far more bewildering than any magical one, and far more terrifying too.'

The man stared intently at Harry. He spoke some more but Harry had stopped listening, too busy think-ing about what he had already heard. *Skills that dazzled us all. Skills that made us think anything was possible.* Deep in his chest, his heart began to throb, and he felt the pulses in the side of his neck twitching to life. Those flickering sensations were back, travelling over his skin. *Just like before a trick.* He knelt there, letting them take him over, and looking into Mr James's eyes.

Then he looked down at Arthur, struggling on the floor.

'Harry?' Billie said. 'What are you doing?'

'Stop!' Mr James tried to grab his arm. 'I have told you: we will take over from this point!'

Harry's hands were back on Arthur's body. His fingers scurried, searched, examined, as Mr James's words echoed in his thoughts. *Skills that dazzled us all . . .* With every echo his hands sped up, diving into pockets, searching along seams. He sent them digging through the lining of the jacket, the fingertips fluttering over the silken material, detecting the tiniest irregularity in the stitching. Mr James grabbed at him, but he pushed him away. He remembered the New York magicians, and how the tiniest sign had given away their secrets to him, and his fingers moved on to his friend's skin, floating over his face, his trembling neck, inspecting that for clues too.

'Maybe we should do as he says, Harry?' Billie tried to grab him too. 'Maybe we should let him take over . . . For Artie's sake.'

'Don't let Artie hear that!' Harry kept searching. 'Remember what Doctor Mincing said—he could be listening to every word. Can't have him thinking we're giving up on him . . . hey, what's that?'

Spatters of purple ink on the cuff of Arthur's sleeve. Some were dry, but a couple smeared Harry's fingertips when he brushed at them. *Still fresh.* There were other wet spatters, now he looked for them, on Arthur's jacket, and his trousers. He stopped searching the body, and checked the nearby floor. *More spatters there too.* He crouched down low, and peered along the floorboards. He saw Arthur's pen, lodged under the base of the bookcase on the left, a short distance away. *The barrel of it, without the lid.* He sprang across and picked it up. Purple ink dribbled from it. Billie stumbled up next to him, and so did Mr James.

'That leaky old pen.' Billie joined him. 'Must have been holding it when it happened.'

'Just like Mayor Monticelso . . . Where's the lid . . . ?'

'What?' Mr James butted in. 'Harry, I must insist you stop this!'

Harry closed his eyes. He saw the soft glow of the office again, the paper-strewn rug. He saw Mayor Monticelso's lidless pen, its ebony carriage, its shining metalwork, clutched in his own fingers. He opened his eyes again, and saw the barrel of Arthur's pen in its place.

'Mayor Monticelso dropped his pen, too. I found it when I was up in his study.'

'Which makes sense.' Billie pointed back at Arthur's flailing arm. 'Arthur, the mayor—they were both having fits, so obviously they'd drop whatever they were holding.'

'Yes but the lid . . .' Harry crouched down by the floor again. 'Where's the lid?'

'Cease this investigation, Harry!' Mr James folded his arms. 'You must leave this matter to us—I demand it! Do you not realize how much danger you are in already?'

Harry saw the lid. It was lodged under a skirting board at the far end of the library, at least fifteen feet away from the pen. *Just like Mayor Monticelso.* He pounced on the lid, held it up and paced back to Arthur's body. Standing over him, he held the pen in one hand, the lid in the other, and his arms arced, miming the throw, just as he had done in Mayor Monticelso's office.

'Just like the mayor. He threw the barrel of the pen in one direction, the lid way off in the other.'

'So?' Billie's face was tear-stained, confused.

'But if they went in two different directions, then they must have been in two different hands, see?'

'But that's just what happens when you use a pen.' Mr James frowned. 'You take the lid off and—'

'And you slot the lid back onto the other end.' Harry performed the action, the lid sliding on with a click. Then he pulled it off again. He looked into it, but it was perfectly empty. 'Or you put the lid in your pocket or something. But you do that pretty quickly.

The length of time you're holding the pen in one hand, the lid in the other—it's a couple of seconds, no more.'

'And?' Billie asked.

'So isn't it a bit unusual that both Artie and Mayor Monticelso got hit by this demon curse or whatever it is at the exact same time? During the few seconds after they opened their pens?'

He held the pen perfectly still. He saw that Mr James was looking at it too.

'An interesting clue, I'll give you that,' he said. 'Proof of your remarkable skills, if any were needed. But still, I insist you leave this investigation to others. I cannot continue to expose you to such danger—'

'Let Harry think, will you?' Billie snapped. She pulled Arthur's pen out of Harry's hand and slid its lid on and off. 'Mind you, you'll have to do quite a bit of thinking, Harry. I can't see it—what can a leaky old fountain pen have to do with a demon curse?'

*The clink of a bottle, the gurgle of liquid.* Harry saw something, a blur of movement down at the end of a nearby aisle of books. He swept down it, the books' spines flashing at him. He kept running until he reached the end of the stacks, and then he turned towards the figure by the door.

It was Doctor Mincing. His briefcase was open, and he had a bottle of fluid in his grip. He was tipping it onto a cloth, and using it to daub at his hand.

On which was a splatter of purple ink.

# Chapter Fifteen

Harry's boots scrabbled at the polished floor as he skidded down the library aisle, but Doctor Mincing had seen him and was too quick. The bottle smashed into a wall, the cloth fluttered through the air and Mincing was by the door, fumbling with the key. He opened it, slid through, and slammed it behind him just as Harry reached it. The key rattled in the lock on the other side. Harry threw himself down on the floor, squinted under the gap, and saw the doctor's shoes scampering towards the main staircase. He stood up, his fingers dancing in his pockets, searching for something to use as a pick. *Won't be quick enough.* He turned, and ran for the windows at the far end of the reading room.

'Where are you going? What's happening?' Billie stumbled along beside him. Tears still trailed over her cheeks.

'Doctor Mincing! We've got to find him!'

'Why?'

'The purple ink from Artie's pen! All over his hand!'

'But are you sure Artie's pen's got something to do with it? We haven't worked that out for sure, have we?'

'How come Mincing was trying to rub the ink off then? How come he ran off as soon as I saw it?'

'True, but—'

'Must have done something with the pen. Put something inside it perhaps . . .'

'COME BACK! COME BACK, BOTH OF YOU!'

Mr James's voice boomed after them. Harry glanced back and saw the tall pale-suited figure striding along the aisle, an arm thrust out. But Harry was already at the window. He pulled the latch, swung the sash open and stepped out onto the ledge. The sky flashed with lightning and rain hurtled down, but Harry's boots kept their grip on the ledge as he helped Billie out through the window too. About seven feet away from the library a fire escape ran down the side of another building. Harry fixed his gaze on it as Mr James's voice boomed through the open window behind him.

'Let others take over from now! You are not ready. Not yet.'

Harry jumped. He flew through the rain, arced between the two buildings, and his outstretched hands caught the fire escape's rail. He swung onto it and threw back an arm just as Billie leapt off the ledge too and plummeted towards him. Her hand reached out, he grabbed it, and she thudded into the fire escape's side. Harry helped her over the rail and together they spiralled down the iron stairs.

'There he is, Billie!' cried Harry, pointing into the rain.

From the fire escape, Harry saw the crowd gathered outside the library. Doctor Mincing was pushing out through the swarming bodies, his bag clutched under his arm, and he hurried down one of the streets that led away. Harry clattered down the rest of the steps and ran after him, dodging between doorways and avoiding brightly lit windows. Billie gripped his hand and he heard her struggling for breath. Together, they kept running, their gaze fixed on the stumbling silhouette ahead.

Droplets of rain snaked into Harry's eyes, blurring his vision, but he wiped them away fiercely. The streets were becoming even darker and the nearby buildings were empty of light.

'What's going on, Harry?' Billie's voice was weak.

'I told you. Doctor Mincing, the pen . . .'

'Not just that—everything!' She pointed back to the library. 'This Mister James, his organization— what's it all about?'

'I don't know.'

'The demon curse—we still haven't worked that out either! What is it?'

'I don't know!'

'Don't know much about anything, do we?'

'We know Arthur's in trouble, and the Islanders too.' Harry tried to keep his voice steady. 'And we know we're going to do whatever it takes to help them. And that's all we need to know for now, isn't it?'

But Harry slipped as he said it. The cobbles were wet and his eyes were filled with rain. He slammed down onto one knee. *It's the shock of what's happened,* he told himself, as he scrambled back up. *The discovery of Arthur in that terrible state, and everything else besides.* He swayed, recovering his balance. He wondered if he had ever felt his heart pound so hard—it was making his whole body shake, and maybe that was affecting his balance too. *Concentrate . . .*

He kept on running.

Harry and Billie chased Doctor Mincing over a narrow bridge. They followed him down a set of stone steps, and started weaving through alleyways, each one narrower than the last. The doctor swerved around a corner. They followed him along a street that seemed to grow muddier with every step, water bubbling around the paving stones.

Reeds grew up through cracks, their leaves dripping with rain. Dark slime trickled out of drains. Harry's balance was back, and he was glad about that, because his boots were heavy, smothered with mud and difficult to move. He saw that the buildings around him were crumbling, and that some of them tilted over, half-sinking into the ooze.

'Thought I knew New Orleans pretty well,' Billie panted. 'But I've never been here before. Looks like it's turning back to swamp.'

A gas lamp glimmered ahead, slanted at an angle. Its light picked out the shape of a crumbling wharf. Doctor Mincing was hurrying along it in the rain, towards a line of old rowing boats. He clambered down into one, and an oil lamp flickered to life in the boat's stern. Mincing tugged at the oars, heading out across a dark stretch of water, a lake thick with weed.

'What is this place?' Billie hissed.

Harry said nothing. He waited until the sound of the doctor's oars vanished into the rain and then made his way out along the wharf. Together, he and Billie stepped down into the nearest boat and set out across the water, Harry pulling the oars, Billie paddling in the prow. Harry saw the flicker of Doctor Mincing's oil lamp, some distance away. He concentrated on rowing, struggling to free the oars of weed. He felt Billie's hand gripping his shoulder.

'What's that up ahead?' Billie hissed again. 'Some kind of prison?'

Harry turned. Doctor Mincing's boat could still be seen and, beyond it, a dark hulk of a building loomed on the lake's far side. Harry rowed harder and looked round again, once the building was nearer. Bars filled the windows, and plants from the lake had wound their way into the thick dark walls. The whole back half of the building had fallen away, leaving a crumbling mess of stone. Out from the building's side a rickety jetty protruded, wooden steps leading down to the lake. Rain spattered off Doctor Mincing's lamp as he moored his boat to the jetty, climbed up the steps, and tottered towards the building's front door. He disappeared inside. As their boat glided up to the jetty Harry made out a wrought iron sign, curving in the rain: *Bolson's Hospital for the Insane.*

'Not a prison then,' said Billie.

'Not quite,' said Harry.

They moored the boat and climbed the rickety steps. Up ahead, light flickered through the asylum's door, faint and yellowed. *Mincing's lamp.* Harry crept towards the door, Billie pressed behind him. He felt the vibrations of her heart, and his own heart was pounding again too, making his shirt twitch against his skin.

He went in.

The light hovered in the distance. Its glow picked out thick cell doors, long rows of them, running off in every direction. Some were shut, others lay partly open with only darkness beyond. Harry kept moving. They passed more cell doors and he stepped into a central hallway, iron walkways hanging overhead. He saw Mincing's oil lamp, left on a desk. Harry flinched as the spindly shape of Doctor Mincing himself flitted in front of the light, clutching something in his arms, the light gleaming off its curves.

It was a jar. There were more of them too, lined up on a row of shelves. Something was moving inside them. Tiny movements caught the light, and shadows flickered near the bottom of every glass shape. Harry looked closer, and gasped. He tried to stifle the noise with his hand, but it was too late.

'You found me! You FOOLS!' Doctor Mincing had spun round, and was staring straight at them. 'I prayed you would not! I did what I could to shake you off! You cannot blame me!'

He stumbled away from the shelves, his arms still wrapped around one of the jars. His shaking was even worse than usual, his every muscle convulsing, and his voice was a strangled cry. Tears trickled from his eyes and Harry noticed that the doctor's hands were still stained with purple ink.

Harry took a step forward and then reached into his jacket. He pulled Arthur's pen from the inside pocket, tugged off the lid and held it up. Then he stared back at the jar.

He could see what was inside.

# Chapter Sixteen

'Stay back! Not a step closer!' Doctor Mincing stumbled away, clutching the jar.

But Harry kept moving forward. He crouched down so that his eyes were level with the jar. Doctor Mincing's fingers scrabbled over the glass but, behind them, Harry saw other shapes scrabbling too. There were about seven of them. Tiny, no more than half an inch long, they scurried so fast that it was hard to tell one from the other: a tangle of scaled bodies, thrashing pincers, spiny limbs catching the light. Harry saw a tail arched over each one of them, a sting quivering at its end, its tip dripping with fluid.

'Scorpions!' Billie gasped.

'From the jungles of Costa Rica!' Doctor Mincing wailed, as he sank into a chair.

Harry looked at the creatures, and at the pen again. Billie was gripping the bars of a cell door, trying to steady herself as she took in the jar's contents. But then she flinched back, and Harry was scrambling back too, because Doctor Mincing had swept the jar upwards, holding it over his head in his quaking hands.

'Scorpions, yes! But not just any scorpions!' Tears ran freely down his face. 'Flee without delay, or I shall dash this jar at your feet and set these creatures upon you! You shall discover their uniqueness then. Just like your friend before you . . .'

'His pen.' Harry held it up. 'You put one of them inside. You did it with Mayor Monticelso's pen too—I found that as well, in his office, nowhere near its lid.' The scorpions were hurling themselves at the jar's sides, venom from their stings spattering the glass. 'You snapped the lid shut. There would be enough space for one inside, although it would have got pretty angry in there.'

'It's impossible!' Billie pointed. 'Scorpions— they're dangerous, sure. They can even kill people. But send people mad, so mad that it's like a demon's taken them over—no scorpion's ever done that. And a sting would leave a mark, wouldn't it? There was nothing on Mayor Monticelso, or on Artie either.'

'These are no normal scorpions! Your friend could confirm that, were he not in their venom's grip.' Doctor Mincing lowered the jar, but kept it tightly clutched in his arms. 'I suspected from the moment you arrived at the mayor's bedside that you were far from being ordinary orphan well-wishers—I know Tobermory Swamp quite well; the accents out there are quite particular, and nothing like yours. So I kept an eye on you—in particular I followed your friend when he made his way to the New Orleans Public Library. I watched him plucking out one book after another, making notes. From the books he chose, I saw how cleverly he was following the evidence . . .'

'But he was in the Magic and Folklore section,' Harry muttered. 'Nothing to do with scorpions . . .'

'He started off in that section, certainly!' Doctor Mincing wailed. 'But his research skills are clearly formidable, because it wasn't long before he was looking through books much further up the aisle, in the Madness and Insanity section, consulting books that I myself have studied long and hard. I knew it would be no time at all before he was scribbling in that notebook about how certain creatures have been discovered, scorpions for example, the venom of which can take over the chemistry of the brain, sending whoever is affected into an agonizing madness, a madness that possesses them utterly.' A blink sent his tears flying, and he clutched the jar tighter. 'I vowed those would be notes he would never make! He had left his pen next to his notebook, back in Magic and Folklore and—'

'You set your trap.' Harry held up the pen. 'Just like you did for Mayor Monticelso.'

'An ingenious trap, I think you'll agree! I watched him as he hurried back, opened his notebook, took the lid off his pen . . .' Doctor Mincing shrugged. 'Then I walked up the aisle and re-shelved the books he had been consulting in Madness and Insanity, all in their correct places. Your friend's writhing body technically belonged in that section too, rather than in Magic and Folklore.' He smiled. 'But it was in my interest to allow myself a small cataloguing error.'

'Why you—' Billie lunged forward, but Harry held her back.

'Let him talk!' He hissed in her ear. 'We've got to find out everything! We'll never help Artie otherwise!'

Harry looked back at Doctor Mincing, who was dropping into a chair, grey tendrils of hair drooping over his face. He placed the jar of scorpions on his desk and started rubbing his left arm just above the wrist, wincing as though in pain.

'What do I care for this business? Mayor Monticelso, your interfering friend—what do I care about either of them? What do I care about what lies *behind* the business, either; it is nothing to do with me! Dark and powerful it may be, and I must do its bidding, but I care nothing for it.' He rubbed his wrist harder, pushing the sleeve up to the elbow. 'You were told, I think, that I have journeyed the world researching diseases of the mind. True, although not since that field trip to the jungles of Costa Rica. Since then, these creatures, that is all I know. Their fluids, their venom, that is all I have become . . .'

His unsleeved arm rested in his lap, its flesh exposed. It was swollen all over with red sores; at the centre of each was an infected pinprick. Darkened blood vessels spread away from the sores. The sleeve remained lifted, and Doctor Mincing stared down at his arm as if it were an object that had nothing to do with him, even as the darkened vessels throbbed, their contents pulsing into his body.

'For twenty years I have tested these creatures. Originally, their poison was weak, however intriguing its effects. But that soon changed, once my studies began. I believed some great medical secret might lie within the venom's chemistry, and I bred the scorpions in order to strengthen that venom, to concentrate its effects. In order to do so, I allowed the creatures to sting me, a task they performed with relish, particularly once my breeding had concentrated the power of their aggression gene. And those stings allowed me to observe the effects of their poison from the closest possible vantage point.' His eyes snapped into narrow slits. 'Clearly, in order not to give way to those effects completely, I had to devise other concoctions from the scorpions' venom, ones that would cleanse my body of its effects, for what use is research if one is never granted a period of calm to write it up? For many years, that process worked, and I studied the venom with ease. But sadly, my body weakened—how could it not, when subjected to poisoning every day? The effects of the venom, no matter how carefully they were swept away, took hold and now my cleansing potions merely reduce those effects on me nothing more.' He lifted his arm. 'The scorpions' stings leave no trace, one of their many ingenuities. Sadly, the process of injecting an antidote over and over again leaves many signs, a great many . . .'

His fingers flexed; the dark vessels swelled under his skin. Harry watched his slitted eyelids, which were bulging with the movement of the eyes behind them. Anger, despair, a strange glee—they each seemed to be gripping Doctor Mincing in turn as he slumped in his chair. *Utterly mad,* thought Harry. But in among all the madness, the doctor had muttered a few words that Harry knew were worth remembering. *Other concoctions . . . An antidote . . .*

'Look at what remains of me!' Mincing held up his arm. 'My body, it is the site of an experiment, no

more. A test-tube scorched through over-use, a laboratory blackened with fumes—if only my discoveries had
been put to noble scientific use, as I once dreamed!
Instead of falling victim to the dark power that con-
trols them . . .'

'You devised other concoctions, that's what you
said just now.' Harry cut him off. 'Cleansing potions
to wipe out the scorpion venom's effects, to cure the
madness?'

'Why, yes. With skill and time, the venom can be
transformed into its opposite.' Doctor Mincing reached
into his pocket. A corner of his mouth twitched into a
smile. 'I have a phial of it right here.'

Billie lunged again. Harry grabbed her, just as
quickly as he had done before. He had seen the small
corked bottle of green liquid in Mincing's fingers, but
he had seen those fingers shift their positions too, until
the glass bottle was held between just two of them,
ready to be dropped at any time. *Too far away to catch*,
Harry calculated, and the asylum floor was unflinch-
ing stone.

'You are right, I have an antidote. Only by injecting a certain dose of the contents of this bottle am
I able to reduce the effects.' Holding the bottle, he
waved at his desk, on which various syringes and nee-
dles could be seen, hanging on a rack. 'For me, in my

weakened state, such a dose merely keeps me alive—but a body affected by merely one sting, such as Mayor Monticelso and your friend, they would no doubt be rid of the disease completely. I am tracking the course of your thoughts correctly?' He looked with one eye through the phial at Harry. Then the fingers adjusted their position. 'Unfortunately, there is not the slightest chance of such a dose being received by anyone, I'm afraid.'

'Don't drop it!' Harry watched the bottle. It was held by the edges of a thumbnail and fingernail, and the floor waited below. *Can't reach it in time.*

'Drop it? It doesn't matter if I do, or don't.' Mincing's jaw dropped open, and a laugh spilled out, its echoes racing through the darkness. 'I tried to bring this matter up before, but you interrupted me. Are you not interested? About what lies behind these scorpions and their venom, every milligram of it? The dark power! The dark power from which there is no escape!'

The fingers around the bottle flexed; the liquid inside swayed.

'Dark power? What are you talking about?' Harry edged forward.

'The power has you in its clutches, whether you know it or not.' Mincing rocked in his chair, the bottle rotating against his thumb. 'Think what this power has made of me and my noble scientific enquiry! Evil, nothing but evil—that is what we have been reduced to, my study and I!' He shook his head. 'Drink the antidote, or smash it on the floor and watch it trickle away; it makes no difference! The dark power will have you in either case. You can be sure of that!'

'What is it?' Harry couldn't listen any longer. 'Tell us! Tell us what it is!'

'*It?* That is your first error.' Mincing kept rocking. '*Her*, that's what you mean—'

A flash of light, the whole asylum thundered, and Harry's hands flew to his ears, trying to seal off the noise. He saw Mincing's rocking had stopped. He was sitting bolt upright, but his head lolled to the side. Then he slumped over, his mouth open, his eyes glazed.

A small red dot grew in the whiteness of his shirt. It darkened, and kept growing. He slithered off his chair, the bottle still between his fingers. His hand hit the floor and the bottle remained intact, cushioned by finger and thumb. Then it rolled onto the floor, and rocked to a halt.

A thud. Harry saw Billie, sprawled face-down beside him. He turned, and made it about halfway round before something slammed into the back of his neck and he too fell forward. He found himself staring at the cold stones of the asylum floor, growing darker and darker, until they were completely black.

# Chapter Seventeen

Harry's eyelids twitched apart. He saw the asylum, its steel walkways, its cell doors, the dark corridor through which he and Billie had entered. And then everything vanished again as he squeezed his eyes shut, wincing at the pain in the back of his head. He tried to reach up and touch it, but his arm wouldn't move.

It was lodged behind his back. Both his arms were. The elbows were trapped by his hip and the wrists were up between his shoulder blades, fixed in place. Harry tried to look round to see what had happened, but then he saw her, standing in a small doorway, right down at the other end of the hall.

A pair of sequin-studded shoes. The bottom of a dress, a mass of interweaving petticoat hems. A pair of spectacles on a stem hovering in front of two eyes. A familiar figure, and she appeared much the same as on the occasions when he had seen her over the last couple of days.

Apart from the jewelled revolver gripped in her left fist.

And the motionless body of Doctor Mincing, upon which one of the sequin-studded shoes was placed.

'My apologies for being ever so slightly late,' Madame Melrose said. 'Were I to have arrived a few minutes earlier, perhaps I could have silenced Doctor Mincing before he told you the information regarding my plan which, now that you know it, makes your fate sadly unavoidable. *Je suis désolée.* By which I mean, *sorry.*' Her fingers twitched around the spectacles' stem, and the lens gleamed. 'Or maybe I don't mean that at all?'

'Harry . . .'

Harry glanced round to Billie. She was just a few inches away, staring desperately towards the corridor that led out to the jetty and their moored boat, and then looking round to take in Madame Melrose, standing in the doorway with Doctor Mincing's body, and the gun. Harry glanced down, and he saw why neither of them could move. They were both strapped into cream-coloured jackets, the cloth thick, heavily stitched, and festooned with buckles and clips, each one of which was tightly fastened. Their arms were drawn up round their backs, their fingers trapped in sewn-up sleeves, and the jackets themselves were padlocked, by steel clips in their collars, to the bars of a cell. Their ankles were tied too, secured by buckled straps.

'Straitjackets, *mes enfants*. What else would you expect, in a deserted asylum?' Madame Melrose slid the revolver into a pocket of her dress. 'A little mouldy after lying unused for several years, and sized for adults, not children. But a few quickly cut extra notches in each buckle strap meant the jackets pulled perfectly tight around your smaller frames. Yes, the straitjackets are capable of their task, namely the restraint of the insane, the demented, the criminally psychotic.' She smiled. 'Or, in this case, the merely over-curious.'

'You!' Billie fought against the straps. 'You're the one behind it! You're the one responsible for what happened to Mayor Monticelso. And Artie too. '

'And let's not forget *l'assassinat de sang-froid*, by which I mean the cold-blooded murder of Doctor Mincing.' The sequinned shoe altered its angle on the corpse. 'He may have been a sinister figure in his own right, but he still counts.'

Harry kept struggling. His wrists were fixed between his shoulder blades, but his hands and fingers flexed in every direction, trying to find a way out. Fighting as hard as he could, gritting his teeth, Harry saw just a single buckle by his left shoulder lift its tooth by a fraction of an inch, but then his strength gave out, and the tooth lowered back again. He stopped to gather his breath, and tried not to look too obviously at the foot of the table nearby, for fear Madame Melrose would follow the direction of his gaze.

The phial of antidote. It lay by the foot of the table leg, just where it had rolled from Doctor Mincing's hand. Blood glistened on the floor, and trailed all the way across the hall to the small doorway where Doctor Mincing's body now lay. It trailed right past the phial, Harry noticed—but there the phial still was. *She's missed it.*

'Mincing, Mayor Monticelso, Artie—why'd you do it, Madame Melrose?' Billie was fighting too, her face flushed, her head thrashing, but her straitjacket wasn't moving either. 'And the Islanders too, remember? Whatever you're up to, they're paying the price, aren't they? I thought you liked them.'

'Liked them? I take a great interest in them, it's true, but that's not the same thing,' Madame Melrose snapped back. 'My interest dates, as I told you, from my youth, when I grew up on a cotton plantation not far from this city. Our workers there were much the same as your Islanders; they had the same colour skin. As do you, I see, *ma jeune fille.*' She looked at Billie. 'So of course I took interest in such folk, their customs and beliefs—why would I not when my family's vast wealth depended on them? They were not only our workers, they were our property. *Nos esclaves.* Our slaves.'

She lifted her shoe from Doctor Mincing's corpse. Its sequins flashed, and her embroidered petticoats rustled as she walked towards them.

'Sadly, our country has changed,' she continued. 'Unlike the slaves in my family's fields, the Islanders aren't useful in themselves, but they *are* useful for something they possess. *La Pointe des Pêcheurs*, I call it.' She looked at them. 'But you'll know it as Fisherman's Point.'

Harry's fingers, arms, and elbows kept struggling on. His body could hardly move but his thoughts made up for it, flying around his head. *Rightfully ours* . . . Daggerbeard's and Yelloweyes' words floated back into his memory, and he studied Madame Melrose and thought how entirely unlike those gnarled fishermen she was, infinitely more elegant—and yet, from what she was saying, every bit as brutal.

'Their land,' he muttered. 'You want them chased off it so you can have it. Just like—'

'Very good, *mon garçon.* But it is one thing to puzzle something out afterwards, another to be the one devising it in the first place.' She smiled. 'Yes, *La Pointe des*

*Pêcheurs* is a most valuable piece of land, conveniently situated on the banks of the Mississippi. Perhaps you have gathered this from that gang of rival fishermen who would be so happy to see the Islanders driven from it? Rumours have reached me of their plots, but I'm afraid there is no chance of *La Pointe* ending up in the hands of, well, fishermen. Our country is changing, *mes enfants.*'

She lowered herself into the chair by the desk. Next to it, a pool of blood from Mincing's body glistened; one of her embroidered petticoat hems settled on it and started drinking the blood up.

'You recall I had a group of gentlemen from Chicago with me when we met at *La Pointe des Pêcheurs*? They weren't *professeurs d'anthropologie sociale*. More useful by far, they were *grands patrons*, businessmen, who wish to buy Fisherman's Point. Fish is still their business, I suppose, but in a far more lucrative way. They seek to build canning factories, to be blunt. Gone will be the days of fishermen living near this city of ours; they can dwell in the swamps, and the fish they find will be brought to sleek new factories, where it will be canned for transportation around the world. A profitable affair, and *les grands patrons* are prepared to pay a considerable fee to whoever can smooth the way towards it being possible. Mayor Monticelso was set against it, you see—to him the Islanders' right to their land was immoveable. But all problems can be solved, with enough thought. And meeting with a diseased and bankrupt doctor of medicine came in handy too.'

Her spectacles tilted across to the corpse in the doorway, dumped at the end of the stripe of blood. She smiled.

'Such fascinating research. I'm sure he told you his intentions were good; he had a habit of saying that. Good, bad, *le bien, le mal.*' She rolled the words off her lips. 'These are subtle distinctions, and not ones that Mincing's diseased brain could easily grasp. He was in a desperate state when I met him—years of failed experiments had left him penniless. I offered to pay for his lodgings, his food, the clothes on his back, in return for him carrying on his scientific work *for me.* I even found him this convenient deserted asylum to use as his laboratory! Occasionally he would express concerns about the way in which I wished to put his scientific discoveries to use, but when I reminded him of his financial dependence on me, he generally became quiet. It is a simple matter, to control a man with no financial means. Even simpler when that man's mind has been overthrown by years of exposure to strange venoms. And it is a simpler matter still, once that man is no longer required, and has become a liability, indeed, to finish with him.'

She noticed the bloodied hem of her petticoat. A frown appeared on her forehead, but she lifted her dresses by the tiniest amount, and resettled on the chair. Harry struggled even harder, his gaze on the phial of antidote. *No way of getting it, no way at all.* The thought hit him suddenly, and his muscles started to shake. Cold, frightened weakness spread through his body as Madame Melrose spoke on.

'*Un tour très simple*, a simple affair, once I had thought it through. Remove Mayor Monticelso's opposition, and not only that—remove the mayor himself, by sending him into a deranged madness. Then devise matters so that the deranged madness would seem to be a creation of the Islanders, allowing the vile Oscar Dupont to stir up a typhoon of rage that would sweep the Islanders from the city, leaving me free to use my council position to guide through the sale of Fisherman's Point to the *grands patrons*, in return for not only my fee but a percentage of all profits. Once again, I shall live in the manner to which I was accustomed on the family plantation! A neat affair—and it will be all the neater once the last details are complete.' Her spectacles swung back to Doctor Mincing's corpse.

'The remains of my accomplice must be taken to the other end of the asylum, to be dumped through a hatch I use for such business—various alligators lurk nearby who will dispose of the body. That just leaves you, *mes enfants.*'

Harry fought against the buckles. Sweat trickled down his face, but the only movement he could see was of the buckle over his shoulder, its tooth rising and settling down. *Impossible.* He stared at Madame Melrose, who was smiling, clearly delighted by the story she had just told. *All of it unknown, unguessed by me.* His muscles grew even weaker as he thought back over everything that had happened. He thought of how skilfully he had searched Arthur's clothes, and found that blot of ink. He thought how determinedly he had followed Doctor Mincing, tracked him down to this dark place. And yet all the time, a deeper mystery had been lurking, one that he hadn't guessed at all. *Missed it . . .*

Harry froze. Madame Melrose had lifted her revolver.

'I expect you are wondering why I didn't shoot you as soon as I found you here, rather than club you with the gun's other end?' The revolver rotated in her hand, muzzle following heel. 'It was quite considered, *mes enfants.* My plans may be conceived at great speed, but they are perfectly precise.'

She was up out of the chair. She had circled Doctor Mincing's desk, and Harry was quite sure she had no idea about the antidote, because she was standing with the bottle almost touching her shoe. But he was more concerned about what she was doing with Doctor Mincing's scorpion-filled jars, taking them down from the shelves, and arranging them next to the one on the desk.

'Oscar Dupont's mob is violent and ugly. But there is no harm, for my purposes, in it becoming more violent and ugly still. And what could better produce that effect than the discovery of two further children, also in the unending grip of the demon curse? *Coup d'éclat!* By which I mean, how very startling.' She turned. 'The pain, I should warn you, is supposed to be excruciating. But you've seen Mayor Monticelso and your dear friend. I don't need to tell you that.'

She tucked the final jar into a leather bag hanging from her shoulder. The rest, six in all, each filled with its furious contents, she left lined up along the desk. Harry saw the scorpions, tiny arched bands of muscles, blur against the insides. He saw droplets of venom trickle down the glass, from wherever the stings had struck.

'I shall keep a few of the specimens for possible further use.' She patted the jar in the bag, and swept back to the doorway across the hall. 'The rest, however, must be disposed of. I shall release them to roam in the swamp. The food they rely on, a rare variety of sugar cane, grows only in Costa Rica, so they will perish in time. However, kind soul that I am, I have left them the last remains of their favourite food *à l'intérieur de vos camisoles de force.*' She arrived at the door, and Mincing's body. 'By which I mean—and it is so very important that you understand me!—inside your straitjackets.'

She spun the spectacles on their stem several times, like a windmill, and then stopped the lenses in front of her eyes. The gun muzzle pointed towards the jars on the desk, and its tip blazed. One of the jars shattered, and Madame Melrose's thumb pulled back the revolver's hammer. Five more shots and the rest of the jars shattered, one by one. Finally, the last shot faded away.

'As mentioned, I must now dispose of my colleague.' Madame Melrose bent down and grabbed one of Doctor Mincing's legs. 'I shall return shortly and, once I am sure the creatures have done their work and scurried away, I shall cut the straitjackets from your contorting bodies and ferry you back to the city, where you will be discovered in some alleyway—further evidence of the Islanders' wickedness.'

'You'll never get away with this!' Billie cried, but her words were blurred by the trembling of her lips.

'*Adieu, mes enfants,*' Madame Melrose said. 'I suspect that needs no translation?'

She lugged Mincing out through the door. The stripe of blood extended, glistening. Another heave, and the door slammed.

Leaving Harry and Billie with the shattered fragments of glass, still rocking on the floor.

And the sound of tiny claws, scuttling towards them.

# Chapter Eighteen

Harry fought against the straps. His arms struggled, his fingers tore at the material, but his muscles were cramping and his movements were slowing down. He wrenched, kicked, and squirmed until he could hardly catch his breath. The straitjacket's neck remained bolted to the bars, and that single buckle down by his shoulder lifted its tooth, but that was all.

*Impossible.*

The scorpions were scuttling through the murkiness, the light from Doctor Mincing's lamp gleaming on their scales. *They've smelt the sugar cane.* Their tiny claws pattered over the stone as they headed towards him and Billie, and he smelt the sweet odour too, wafting up out of his straitjacket's insides. His tongue was dry; his whole body shuddered.

*No idea what to do.*

'Keep trying, Harry!' Billie's voice was a strangled hiss.

'I . . . I can't . . . He tried to fight, but his muscles cramped even more. 'These jackets—they're made for mad people, aren't they? Even someone crazy wouldn't be able to get out. How can I—?'

'The scorpions! If they sting us—'

'I know!'

'It's not just us! Artie, Mayor Monticelso—we've got to save them! The Islanders too!'

'I know that!'

'The antidote!' She managed to jolt her head towards the phial, lying by the desk.

'I know.'

'We've got to—'

Her voice cut out and Harry saw why. The first scorpion had crept onto the hem of her dress, and was making its way towards her straitjacket. The tiny tail, with its venom-dripping sting, arched above it, quivering at every fold of cloth the scorpion encountered. Something twitched against Harry's leg, and he glanced down to see three scorpions crawling up the outside of his trousers. Only his eyes moved as he watched the scaly creatures journeying up his body. They crawled onto his straitjacket and weaved through the buckles and straps. Two more crept onto the trouser leg, following the others' path. His body was frozen but he could feel his heart hammering inside, as if it was trying to fight its way out. He thought of all the tricks he knew, all the last-minute escapes he had pulled off, here in New Orleans, back in New York too. *None of it matters,* he thought.

Because he had never been truly frightened until now.

'Please Harry, keep trying . . .' Billie's voice could hardly be heard. 'Remember what he said . . . The man in the pale suit . . . Mr James . . . Back in the library . . .'

Harry's eyes slid sideways to see several more scorpions on Billie: five on her dress, another three halfway along her arm. Another was up by her strait-jacket's collar, and it crept over the stitched edge and disappeared inside. Her voice weakened, and Harry knew she was trying not to move the muscles of her neck.

'Who knows who he is . . . Who knows what the Order of the White Crow is either . . . But I heard what he said back there . . . About you.' She angled her eyes towards him. 'About your skills. *Miraculous*, he called them. *Skills that make anything seem possible.* Me and Artie, we impressed him too, but you Harry, you were the one who dazzled him.'

'It's no good . . .'

He tried to remember it too. He closed his eyes and tried to bring it back to life, that moment in the library when all had seemed lost, and Mr James's words had sent energy racing back through him. *But it's no good now.* Even if Mr James was here, whispering about his skills right in his ear, it would have no effect. Besides, Mr James had said other words too, and those were the ones Harry could hear perfectly clearly, lingering in his thoughts.

'He didn't just talk about my skills. He said we weren't ready, remember?'

'What?'

'The investigation was too difficult. That's what he said. He'd made a . . . misjudgement . . .'

'I know but—'

'He was right, wasn't he? Look at us!'

The scorpions were all over his trousers, the straitjacket too. He looked at those arms and legs, and remembered how quickly he had clambered up inside the dumb waiter shaft at City Hall. He saw one of his boots, and remembered how he'd kicked the sack of charms into the brazier's flames. He remembered his fingers, cleverly picking the lock of a suitcase when he was trapped inside . . . *But none of it makes any difference now.* Here he was, that nimble, skilful body, unable to move at all . . .

'I believe in you, Harry, even if you don't. Mr James was right about your skills; it doesn't matter what else he said. That's the truth. Artie would say the same.'

A scorpion was on Harry's face. He felt it scuttle across his forehead, and almost straightaway he felt another one creep onto his cheek. He froze, and for a few seconds those terrible pattering sensations were all he could feel, all he could think of. But then, even as he lay there, he realized that Billie was still speaking, and he listened to her words, every single one of them.

'Obviously, I wouldn't normally say this—don't want you to get big-headed or anything . . .' Her voice was almost gone. 'But it really is true. What you do . . . There's no one else who can do anything like it. Harry, are you listening . . . ?'

Harry slanted his eyes to the side. He saw Billie's face again, and shuddered at the sight. For a start, there were the scorpions crawling over it. But worst of all, for him, was that desperate hint in her expression, of hope.

*Hope in me.*

'Whatever it takes, you always do it,' Billie kept going. 'Why, just yesterday morning on the Crescent Express, you rescued me and Artie out of those suitcases, didn't you?'

'Yes but . . .' Harry felt scorpions inside his strait-jacket, their claws against his skin.

'When we pulled in at the station, two minutes later, you were doing the Fiery Coal Dance.'

'I know, but—'

'As soon as I knew the Islanders were in trouble, I asked you to help . . . I knew you'd say yes. I knew you'd do whatever it took to save them.'

'I can't . . .' He felt one creep down his spine.

'You always do it, Harry. You always manage to win through. And you'll do it now, yeah? You'll get us out of here. For Artie . . . For Mayor Monticelso . . . For the Islanders . . . For me . . .'

Her words stopped. The scorpions on her face had reached her lips, and not even she dared speak any more. The insects stood right by her mouth, their stings quivering, and Billie was silent, her eyes wide with terror. But her words kept echoing in Harry's mind. *If only those words could change things*, he thought, as he looked at his straitjacket. There were countless scorpions on it. Inside, he felt a crowd of them gathering at a spot just under his ribs. *Too late* . . . He tilted his head back and looked, for what he thought might be the very last time, at his friend, lying there in a strait-jacket, just a few inches away . . .

*Just a few inches away.*

Harry's heart stopped beating. He waited, and felt it jolt back to life, pounding even harder. He wondered if the vibrations would disturb the scorpions but, so far, they seemed just to be creeping further on their journeys. He looked at the ones on the outside of the jacket, weaving their way between the buckles. He looked at the particular part of the jacket he was interested in: the strap by his left shoulder.

*With the buckle that had lifted its tooth.*

A scorpion was crawling over it, lifting its spiny legs. Harry waited for it to move on, and turned his head until he was staring at Billie.

'The straitjackets . . . They're for mad people, yes?'

'You said that. I know.' There were fewer scorpions on Billie's face, but she seemed hardly to have the strength to whisper.

'Even someone in a mad fit couldn't get out, yes?'

'You've said this, Harry . . .'

'But people who are mad, they're on their own, aren't they? All locked up in their own craziness.'

'I suppose so. But—'

'They wouldn't listen to anyone. Wouldn't matter how good a friend they were, wouldn't matter what they said . . .'

'Harry?'

Harry looked back at the buckle. He concentrated on the scorpions inside the jacket, working out where they were. Most of them had gathered at the spot beneath his ribs. *Some of the cane sugar's there, perhaps.* He felt them in other places too—his neck, his chest—but there were some bits of his body that were free of them: his left arm, for example. *Very slow.* Gritting his teeth, he tightened that arm until it was pushing against the straitjacket as hard as it could. No other part of his body moved, only the arm. His eyes stayed fixed on the buckle.

'Harry? What are you doing?'

The buckle's tooth lifted. It rose only a tiny amount, but Harry kept it like that, the muscles in his arm shaking. Inside the jacket, around the rest of his body, he felt the scorpions go still. But they didn't sting. *Not yet.* One by one, they continued with their scuttling, burrowing onwards. Beads of sweat ran down Harry's face; as his arm remained clenched, the buckle's tooth remained raised. He started to roll to the side.

'Harry! Careful! The scorpions, they'll—'

*Just like a trick.* Control was everything. Harry rolled his body so slowly that it hardly seemed to be moving at all, the scorpions on the outside of the jacket crawling on as if nothing was happening, the ones inside undisturbed too. But he *was* moving, he could tell that by focusing on that lifted tooth and watching the bars of a nearby cell door move past behind. He watched that tiny, inch-long piece of metal as it traced an arc, down to the nearest buckle on Billie's straitjacket.

'Stay still.' His lips shaped the words.

He could only use one eye now. One of the scorpions on his face was creeping over the lid of the right one, so he concentrated on what he could see with the other eye instead. More muscles tightened, and the lifted tooth of the buckle glided forward, sliding into the buckle on Billie's jacket. It hooked under the leather strap, and angled itself against that buckle's tooth. Harry rolled slightly back, and watched one tooth lever the other upwards.

The tooth of Billie's buckle lifted.

And slid out of the hole of its strap.

'Your turn. But slowly.' Harry hissed, keeping still. 'Undo one of my buckles . . . any one . . .'

Billie's arm was already moving. The fallen-away strap had released a fold of material and, although the arm was buried in the jacket, it could shuffle about. Harry watched it struggle beneath the cloth. Billie's face was pouring with sweat and he knew that she would be feeling those tiny bodies creeping over her, but her arm managed to re-position itself, her hand pushing its way out. Harry saw two fingers poke out through a gap, and strain towards one of the buckles on Harry's jacket. They brushed against it, and fell away. Billie tried again and this time the fingers grabbed the buckle's strap and pulled.

The buckle's tooth slid out of the strap. Harry could move his shoulder, but nothing more.

*That's all I need.*

Harry's shoulder wriggled loose and his elbow hinged upwards. He could feel the scorpions feeding all over him, but he moved so smoothly that none of them seemed to notice. *Control.* The jacket was looser, his wrist flexed and his fingers probed around. He managed to wiggle one of his fingers out of the straightjacket, hinged it back and flicked a buckle free. His hand was out, and it swept about, finding buckles all over the jacket, sliding them loose. The rest of his body lay still, the scorpions undisturbed. His hand took hold of the jacket's front edge, and opened it up. He looked down at his body, inside.

Scorpions were all over it, but they were all over the inside of the jacket, too. Harry saw pieces of sugar cane clinging to the jacket's insides, and noted how the scorpions were gathered around those specks. *Food, that's what they want most.* He watched the scorpions on his body scuttle about, and make their way back into the folds of the jacket that lay around him.

Slowly, he sat up. His arms slid from the jacket's sleeves and he felt the scorpions scuttle away from his neck, his back, vanishing down into the jacket, their sugar-laced nest. He gathered his legs underneath himself and stood up, the final scorpions creeping down his trousers. He waited until the last one was gone, and crouched over Billie.

'Don't move,' he whispered. 'My turn again.'

Billie did exactly as he asked. His hands rustled around the buckles of her jacket. Opening her jacket, he watched the scorpions hurry away from her body into the sugary folds. He grabbed her arms, pulling her so that she rose up out of the jacket, leaving the scurrying hordes behind. Only then, as her face grew close to his, did she allow herself to move a little, her lips shaping the words.

'I knew you could do it, Harry . . . You always do . . .' she whispered.

'OW!'

Pain shot into Harry's hand. Something tore through his skin, just beneath the base of his thumb, but he kept his grip on Billie until he had lifted her free. Harry rotated his wrist and saw it, the scorpion, scurrying over his knuckles. He flung it away, but the pain was already travelling deeper into his hand. He felt it, a cruel jabbing, racing up through his wrist.

Harry gripped his arm in a desperate attempt to choke off the flow of blood, but the pain travelled on, up his shoulder, into his neck. Gathering strength, it burst into his head. Harry fell to his knees, his body slammed onto the floor, and he was lying on his side, jolting all over.

*So this is it. The demon curse.*

It was as if the scorpion's claws were inside his skull, tearing at the flesh inside. The claws were burning hot, and their jagged tips buried themselves into a spot behind his eyes, another one at the base of his neck. Harry felt his back arch, and saw his wrists and arms flex. His whole head pulsed with the pain.

*No demon,* he told himself. *Only pain. But what demon could ever be as terrible as this?*

The claws dug, twisted, scraped. His arms flailed, his head twisted to the side. A few feet away, he saw a fragment of one of the glass jars, and he saw, in its curved surface, the reflection of his face. The muscles were stretched wide, the teeth bared. He hardly recognized himself, and then he recognized himself even less, as the claws dug again, and his face became a blur. He closed his eyes. The claws kept ripping through the tissue inside his skull, and every rip released a terrible sight.

A gun, flashing with light.

A pen lid, lodged against the foot of a chaise longue.

A glass jar, clutched in two shaking hands.

A flower of blood, spreading over Doctor Mincing's shirt.

Madame Melrose's spectacles, glimmering . . .

The claws dug on. He noticed a new pain, a different one, down in his left arm. A smaller jab, followed by a cool sensation spreading towards his shoulder. A different pain, and not nearly so powerful. He opened his eyes and looked down, to see what it was.

Billie was holding his arm. In her other hand, she clutched one of the syringes from Doctor Mincing's desk. Its needle was buried just beneath his shoulder, its vessel full of the green antidote, and she was pushing the stopper all the way in.

# Chapter Nineteen

Chemicals flooded up Harry's arm. He felt them in his blood, flowing into every part of him. They pulsed in his neck, and he knew they had reached his brain because the claws were releasing their hold. But he could still feel their tips, hot and jagged, and his body shook. Sprawling, he watched Billie pull the needle out of his arm.

'How did you know how to do an injection?' The words struggled out of his mouth.

'Did a stint as a hospital worker, back in Kansas City when I was on the road to New York—didn't I ever tell you about that?' Billie held up the syringe, and the bottle of antidote. 'Just mopping the wards, but I used to watch the nurses give plenty of injections, so I pretty much know what to do.'

'But . . . how did you know . . . the right amount to use . . .' Harry winced, as the claws pushed back.

'Didn't. Still, this syringe's got a green stain up to the seven-fluid-ounce mark.' Billie tapped the syringe. 'And I guessed Mincing used it to give himself a dose. Bit of a risk—but you're used to taking those, aren't you?'

A corner of her mouth curved up, the beginnings of a smile, and she jerked a thumb towards a spot a short distance away. Using all his strength, Harry pushed himself up onto his elbows and saw the shapes of the two straitjackets, their necks still chained to a cell door. Scorpions scurried over them. He felt his own mouth curve too. *One heck of a trick.* He slumped back down, but he felt a warmth across his back, and saw that Billie had caught him. He looked up. He saw his reflection in her eyes, just as he had in the fragment of glass. His face was shivering, he noticed, but that little curved smile could still be seen.

'You did it . . .' Billie whispered. 'And we've got enough antidote for Mayor Monticelso and Artie too.'

'We did it together.' Harry heard his own quavering voice. 'We—'

He stopped. His vision was blurring again, his body slumping back onto the floor. Billie's eyes had turned away, her mouth falling open as the asylum flashed with light. Thunder throbbed, and Harry clutched at his head. The claws were back.

'So you think you have escaped, *mes enfants?*'

Madame Melrose stood in the doorway at the far end of the asylum, the leather bag containing the jar of scorpions hanging from her shoulder, the revolver gripped in her hand. Its muzzle blazed, making the asylum thunder again and something whined past Harry's ear. He saw sparks shower off a cell door to his left, as a bullet ricocheted off it.

'Mincing is disposed of. I see some work remains regarding the two of you.'

'Run, Harry! Run!'

Harry's body lurched upwards. Billie's hands were under his arms, and his boots scrabbled against the stone floor, but the claws were still in his head. *The antidote must take time to work*, he thought, as he and Billie toppled towards the corridor through which they had entered the asylum's hallway. They plunged down it. Another shower of sparks, another bullet whined, but they were out on the wooden jetty, stumbling towards the steps that led down to the boats. Rain pounded off the jetty, and Harry slithered and lost his balance. Billie caught him, and pulled him down the last few steps to where their boat was tied.

'Looks like we're not finished with the risks yet,' Billie was saying. 'Mind you, that's probably how you like it, isn't it? Keep us all on the edge of our seats, right to the very end . . .'

Billie's voice gave way. Harry saw the smile had vanished from her face. She pulled him off the bottom step into the boat, where he sprawled out in the rain. The claws kept pushing back, ripping, tearing. *Get up. Recover.* He heard the splash of oars, and he knew Billie was rowing them away. But Harry also saw, through the rain, the shape of Madame Melrose appearing at the top of the jetty steps.

'Do you really believe you can get away?!' Her voice shrieked after them. One hand reached down and stroked the corked top of the jar of scorpions, protruding from her bag. 'Doctor Mincing's creatures may have failed to dispose of you, but do you really believe my bullets will not find you, as you paddle your *petit bateau*?! My marksmanship is formidable, *rappe-lez-vous*?!'

She reloaded the gun. Harry saw the revolver's carriage swallowing the bullets as Madame Melrose pushed them in. The carriage snapped back, spun, came to a halt. Billie pulled at the oars, but she wasn't fast enough. From a pocket in her dress, Madame Melrose pulled out her spectacles on their stem. She twirled them four or five times, and then they stopped. Rain dripped from them, but the eyes behind were clear.

The muzzle flashed, altered its angle, and flashed again. Harry felt the boat shudder twice and heard Billie cry out. He swung round, and saw that both the oar brackets had been hit, one shot off completely, the other hanging by a single screw. Billie had already thrown one of the oars into the boat, and was trying to use the other as a paddle, but it was too long, and the boat was hardly moving. Harry reached for the other oar, but the claws kept digging. *Get up.* He saw Madame Melrose, her revolver gleaming, the bag containing the scorpion jar swinging at her side. She was descending the rain-covered jetty steps, water flying up around her sequinned shoes.

'You are within range, *mes enfants.* My bullets will find you. True, I am disappointed that your bodies cannot be found trembling with the demon curse. Instead, those two bodies must simply do as the remains of Doctor Mincing have done, and become food for the creatures of the swamp.' The spectacles twirled faster, and she was almost dancing as her shoes splattered on down the steps. 'Ah well—I must content myself with that.'

'Help me, Harry!'

Billie was thrusting the other oar at him. Harry fumbled for it but lost his grip, the oar splashing into the water. The claws pushed even deeper into his brain. *Impossible.* He lay there shaking in the boat, looking back through the rain at the figure on the jetty.

He saw something.

A sequinned shoe slipping. Water splattering, Madame Melrose slithering down onto one knee. The leather bag containing the scorpion jar sliding from her shoulder and slamming onto the step. Harry heard something too.

The crack of glass.

'Look, Billie!'

Harry managed to lift an arm and point. Billie swung round, and froze. She too was staring at the leather bag, lying on the steps. Harry saw a curved fragment of glass jutting from it, and other pieces of glass scattered nearby. Madame Melrose was trying to struggle back up, reaching for the nearby rail while flailing at something on the lower part of her dress. Harry saw a shape scurrying along the blood-soaked hem of her petticoat. Another one higher up her corseted waist. Another on her lace sleeve.

'The scorpions!' Billie cried.

Harry's hands were around his head again. However vital the events at the end of the jetty were, he found it hard to keep his eyes focused. He saw Madame Melrose's back arching. He watched her arms shoot up above her, scrabbling at the air, the revolver falling away. The flesh of her face stretched wide. Harry's eyes flickered shut. But he managed to open them again as he heard the terrible cry, and the splash.

Madame Melrose had tipped off the jetty. The water churned up, a white mass. Lace-covered arms fought, hands thrashed in the foam. Harry saw a face, the eyes bulging, swamp water pouring out of the mouth.

His own eyelids drooped. Everything went dark.

Harry forced his eyes open again. The water still surged up by the jetty, but not so high. He saw a hand, its fingers clawing the rain, and he heard Billie screaming.

His eyes closed. This time, it took him even longer to force them open again.

The water by the jetty still rippled, but only with the rain. White flecks spattered up from each raindrop, forming a pale mist. Apart from that, and the dim light from the asylum, there was blackness all around.

His eyes closed once more and everything went blacker still.

# Chapter Twenty

Harry's eyes sprang open. This time to a blinding light.

The walls around him were white and gleaming; the ceiling above him was perfectly white too, apart from a few cracks slanting through the glare. Harry looked down and saw something else that was white, a strip wound across his body. He tried to move, but it held firm. He stared back at the wall, his eyelids flickering shut.

'Harry?'

His eyes managed to open again. There were shapes in the brightness now, two of them, dark but growing in size. Staring at them made his eyes hurt less, so he kept watching them as they drew close. The gleaming walls seemed to have faded, and he saw other shapes nearby too: framed pictures, a window filled with blue sky. Harry saw that the strip of white was just a folded-back bed sheet, tightly tucked. He pushed and felt it slide loose, and he realized that one of the dark shapes had reached out to help him.

'You'll come round properly soon enough. You got a particularly big shot of scorpion venom, it turns out—one dose of the antidote wasn't enough. Still, I did my best—that stint of floor-mopping in the Kansas City hospital came in handy, yeah?'

Billie was now sitting on the bed. Harry's eyes were wide open at last, and he could make out the room properly, but his gaze remained fixed on his friend. She was smiling back at him as she took one of his hands in hers. Harry's mouth opened to say something but nothing came out. He had noticed another shadowy figure sitting next to the bed and he could only think of that.

He recognized the familiar tweed suit, a tie, a pair of hands holding a book.

'Billie's right, Harry. There's no need to worry. The antidote will see you through in the end—I should know, shouldn't I?'

*Arthur.* That face was its normal thoughtful self, no longer stretched out of shape. Harry searched it for the slightest tremor, but there was none. Those arms, once thrashing blurs, were calmly at his side, and his hands were paging neatly through the book, the title of which Harry could just about make out: *Theories of Animal Venom.*

'Clever and sinister stuff.' Arthur tapped a page of the book, then lifted up an object that Harry recognized as his friend's leaky fountain pen. 'I'd pretty much worked it all out, that night in the library. Found this book, and a couple of others, which explained it all, and so when I took off my pen lid and saw what was crawling out of it I knew what I was in for. Thought I was pretty much finished.' He winced, and then smiled at Harry. 'But it turns out the clever, sinister business wasn't quite clever and sinister enough, was it? Thanks to you, Harry—OOF!'

Harry was up out of the bed. His body was still weak, but somehow he had flung himself forward, and his arms were around Arthur, hugging him tight. Arthur hugged him back and, as he did so, Harry felt a little of his strength return. From a different direction, he felt Billie reach in and join the hug too.

'We did it, Harry,' she whispered in his ear. 'You, me, Artie—not to mention pretty much every doctor in New Orleans, working day and night to make sure you were okay. They brought you right here to City Hall, to work on you alongside Mayor Monticelso, and Arthur too. And you pulled through, Harry—I knew you would.' She laughed. 'Reminds me of the time I had to spend two days in bed after walking non-stop from Ironville, Kentucky to Parkersburg, Virginia . . . I bet you've missed my tales of the road, haven't you?'

Her face was next to Harry's, tears glistening on it, but she was grinning, too. Harry blinked, and he realized he could see perfectly clearly at last—his friends, and everything else in the room. He touched his head with his fingertips, remembering those terrible claws. But they were gone, he was sure of it.

'Mayor Monticelso . . .' At last, he spoke. 'Is he all right?'

'He's fine—just down the corridor, actually.' Arthur shrugged. 'He says he'll come and see you when you're better . . . Harry, wait!'

But Harry was already up off the bed. Billie and Arthur were trying to hold him back, but he was sliding on his clothes, shuffling his boots onto his feet. A couple of unsteady steps and he was out of the room, his friends running along beside him. Harry recognized the curved door at the end of the corridor and made his way there. *City Hall.* The door flew open and he stumbled into a room he knew he had been in before, although it no longer had a bed at its centre. He heard a voice, and he saw an elderly figure sitting in a chair at the room's far end.

'Welcome, my friends. My friends, to whom I owe so very much . . .'

Mayor Monticelso. Harry glanced at the painting on the wall. It still hung there, and this time there was no reason to double-take between it and the face it depicted, because it was a perfect likeness. Those worn but kindly features stared down out of the oils, and the face of the figure in the chair was worn but kindly too, all hint of terror gone. Only a gentle smile quivered on it as the old man rose from his chair and tottered towards Harry with the help of a cane.

'Thank goodness my recovery is complete. For I need every ounce of energy and fitness to express my gratitude once again.' Mayor Monticelso's eyes shone. 'Already I have expressed the utmost admiration for young Billie, who supplied the doctors with the antidote that rescued me from my terrible ordeal!'

'Like I've said, it was no trouble, sir.' Billie curtsied.

'Then I conveyed my immense thanks to Arthur, whose investigations led to his own near-demise, but also to the start of the unravelling of this appalling plot!'

'Please don't mention it, Mister Mayor.' Arthur performed a neat bow.

'Yet still further thanks are needed. For now I meet the boy who performed the most extraordinary task of all.' Mayor Monticelso turned to Harry. 'And I am not the only one who will wish to thank you, young Harry! Come with me.'

The old man grabbed Harry's sleeve. He tugged it with surprising strength, his cane tapping the floor as he headed towards one of the room's several doors, pushed open the door and beckoned Harry in.

'He is here, my friends! Young Harry is here!'

Auntie May sat on a chaise longue while Brother Jacques occupied a leather armchair. All around the room, more of the Islanders were seated, some of them muttering amongst themselves, others paging through newspapers. Most wore their usual fishing clothes, although a few of the men sported ties and jackets, and Auntie May wore a hat with a ribbon round it. She was holding a cup of tea on a saucer, stirring a spoon in it, while Brother Jacques read the *New Orleans Post*, peering through a pair of wire spectacles. He and Auntie May looked up as the Mayor and Harry came into the room.

'The agony of the scorpion's sting!' The old man tottered across to the chaise longue and sat down beside Auntie May. 'But my sufferings would have been ten times greater, a hundred times greater, had I known about the dreadful scheme of which my agony was a part. You Islanders, accused!' He shook his head.

'Thank goodness the plot was so spectacularly foiled.'

'Yes indeed.' Auntie May nodded.

'You are a great friend of ours, Mister Mayor.' Brother Jacques adjusted his spectacles. 'But we Islanders have other great friends too, it turns out. And this boy Harry—he's turned out to be one of them, that's the truth.'

'It wasn't just me.' Harry's voice was still unsteady. 'Billie and Arthur, they—'

'Sure they did.' Brother Jacques leant forward in his chair. 'Billie is a friend of ours from way before, and young Arthur's proved his friendship. Mind you, I'd say we had other help too in this business: the help we Islanders always get in times of trouble. Help that turned out even more powerful than the help of friends . . .'

His deep, dark eyes stared at Harry, who swayed slightly on his feet. The claws had gone, but he still felt a little weak as he listened to Brother Jacques' words. He remembered the brass jars, with the snakeskin, feathers and seeds inside, and he remembered the smoke, sprawling off in different directions, filling his eyes, making them sting. *Maybe the spirits did protect me.* He blinked, and swayed again, but felt two hands grab hold of him, and hold him steady. It was Billie, keeping him up.

'Madame Melrose?' Harry remembered. 'Is she . . .?'

'Drowned in the swamp, we believe.' Auntie May shook her head, stirring her tea again. 'Now that was another friend of ours, or so she said. But she won't be taking us in with her fine words any longer.'

'She certainly won't.' Beside her on the chaise longue, Mayor Monticelso's kindly features darkened. 'The victim of her own violence in two ways. First, she suffered an attack by her own vicious creatures. Second, she had shot off the oar brackets on your boat, making it impossible for young Billie to row back and throw her a rope or the like. So she perished. Her body hasn't been found, mind, but the alligators explain that.' He winked. 'Assuming they hadn't eaten their fill after devouring the corpse of that deranged doctor . . .'

'Mincing.' Harry saw a spot of blood, spreading on a shirt.

'Dead, dead, extremely so. And at first that seemed to be a problem.' Servants were serving more cups of tea, and Mayor Monticelso accepted one before waving the trolley on towards Harry. 'How were we to rid this city of the rumours regarding the Islanders, without the two criminals themselves to account for their crimes? But we need not have worried. Madame Melrose craftily covered her tracks, but Doctor Mincing's notes on his scorpion work remain, throughout which are peppered increasingly demented references to his demonic employer. One glimpse of them set the hideous Oscar Dupont packing his bags, his attempt to ride to office on a storm of viciousness in ruins, I'm pleased to say.' He waved a hand at one of the copies of the *New Orleans Post* that the Islanders were reading. 'The newspapers have carried the true story in full and, with luck, that nasty mob will have learnt the lesson of jumping so quickly to conclusions. A cautionary tale.'

'The fishermen?' Harry asked. 'The ones who tried to put the spirit charms under the floorboards?' One last memory flickered. 'What about their plans?'

'Ah, they don't hate the Islanders any less, I fear.' The mayor tutted. 'But their hatred is now of little concern. I had no hesitation in revealing details of their feeble but manipulative plot to the *New Orleans Post*, and that story is covered too. It is unlikely anyone in this city will be listening to anything they say, on any matter, for some years to come. Again, a cautionary tale.'

A servant pushed a cup and saucer into Harry's hand. He managed to hold it steady as the tea was poured, the golden liquid glowing in the sunlight. Somewhere nearby, he heard a telephone ringing. Harry realized that, in the few minutes since he had regained consciousness, people had been talking to him almost non-stop, an endless stream of revelations and observations and discoveries. *And it's not finished yet*, he told himself, as he turned towards Auntie May, who was saying something in his ear.

'Brother Jacques is right in what he says. The ritual we performed, it summoned the spirits and they protected you, helped you; we are quite sure of it. How else could you have survived as you did? And we believe the spirits may have worked in other ways too, ways that we understand much less.' Her voice dropped even lower. 'After all, is it not strange that you, all three of you, arrived in New Orleans at the very time you did?'

'The spirits work in many ways, it is true.' Brother Jacques looked over his spectacles at Harry. 'And their influence spreads far. Far beyond this city, far beyond this state of Louisiana too.'

'As far as New York, maybe?' Auntie May continued. 'Who knows how they found you? Who knows how they arranged for the three of you to meet, and for you all to arrive in New Orleans at the very time you were most needed? Is it not strange that, at that very time, Billie returned to us? Not only that, but she returned with two friends, each able to help us in their own extraordinary way?'

'The spirits' workings cannot always be understood,' Brother Jacques muttered.

'Indeed they cannot. We can talk round in circles and still we won't make head or tail of their ways. Who knows how they brought you here, all three of you?' The old woman leant forward, and gently took hold of Harry's chin. 'But I'm glad they did.'

Her hand cupped his face. Those eyes stared into him, surrounded by complicated wrinkles. For a moment, Harry found himself almost believing the Islanders' words, their explanation for how he and his friends had arrived in New Orleans. *Hardly stranger than everything else.* But he reminded himself that there was another explanation too and, at the same time, he noticed that the telephone ring he had heard a few moments before had cut out.

A door opened and one of servants edged in, bowing in the direction of Mayor Monticelso before nodding in Harry's direction.

'Telephone call for Harry and his friends, Mayor Monticelso.'

# Chapter Twenty-one

Harry picked up the telephone and Billie and Arthur leant close. The voices of Mayor Monticelso and the Islanders wafted down the corridor, but Harry concentrated on the crackles of static drifting out of the ebony earpiece.

'My congratulations on your remarkable feat,' Mr James said. 'And my apologies for my uncertainty when we last met, regarding whether you should proceed. Mind you, I had good reason because things were hardly going to plan . . .'

'I can see you,' said Harry.

The telephone was by the window and Harry had been looking through the glass, down at the street below, from the moment Mr James had started to speak. There he was, in his pale suit, stood below the iron balcony of the building across the street. A wire from the telephone he was holding stretched through a doorway, a packed suitcase stood by his side, and a horse-drawn cab waited by the curb.

'Yes—a further necessary subterfuge, I am afraid.' Mr James glanced up at the window. 'I deliberately asked to be put through to this extension, so that I could observe you as we spoke. I might have guessed that you would seek to observe me too. Still, observing will be the limit of it.' A gesture at the waiting cab. 'Should you move from the window, I will be gone. If you were in your usual condition, even that might not be fast enough, but I'm calculating the scorpion venom still weakens you.'

'*I'm* still pretty quick though, aren't I?' Billie grabbed the telephone. 'Tell us what's going on or I'll—'

Harry reached out, steadying her while Arthur gently drew the telephone from her grip, angling the earpiece so that they could all hear. Harry kept watching Mr James, but the man in the pale suit hadn't shifted his position at all. For now, it seemed, he was happy to remain. Harry waited with his friends for the voice to crackle out of the telephone again.

'What's going on, Billie? I wish I could be clearer on that subject but secrecy is vital and I can only tell you what you already know: namely that I work for the Order of the White Crow, an organization devoted to—'

'*The overthrow of evil, wherever it may lie,*' Arthur murmured. 'Yes, we know that.'

'The overthrow of evil and, just as important, the rescuing of those threatened by that evil! The Islanders of Fisherman's Point are not alone, I fear, in falling victim to wicked forces beyond their control. There are more like them, many more.' Static swirled back around the voice. 'So, yes, a somewhat out of the ordinary organization. Then again, you yourselves are somewhat out of the ordinary too. Consider what has taken place in the last couple of days alone. Amongst other things, you have disguised yourselves as swamp-school orphans, escaped from a brutal gang of fishermen, discovered scientific secrets in the Madness and Insanity section of the City Library, detected a highly hard-to-spot clue involving a leaky fountain pen and then, of course, pulled off a truly remarkable escape from straitjackets filled with nearly a hundred of the most dangerously poisonous scorpions known to humanity. Given such skills, can you seriously expect to be employed by an organization that is remotely normal? I think not. Unusual people need unusual work, that's what I say.'

*Fair enough,* thought Harry. Glancing at his friends, he sensed that they were thinking the same. Arthur was nodding thoughtfully, Billie had tilted her head on one side, and both of them, noticing he was looking at them, looked straight back, and smiled. He smiled too. He realized his strength was returning quite quickly now, his balance was back, his muscles were steady. He lifted his right hand and flexed the fingers. He watched them darting, angling, each one alive with its own energy.

'I have no doubt said too much,' Mr James was saying. 'My instructions are simply to inform you that, should you so wish, your services are still very much desired by the Order of the White Crow. As mentioned, there will be more who, like the Islanders of Fisherman's Point, require help from you and your remarkable abilities. Now, I think it is time this telephone call ended, although you might like to inspect the telephone itself.'

The earpiece went dead. Harry saw, down across the street, Mr James hand his own telephone to a waiting servant and step into the horse-cab, which rattled away. Glancing out through the window, Harry looked for drainpipes or ledges, but he knew Mr James was right: his strength hadn't returned completely enough for that. *It won't be long though.* He looked back at his hand and watched his fingers moving faster. He realized he could feel his heart too, throbbing gently in his chest, as he listened to Billie and Arthur.

'What was all that about?' said Billie.

'Couldn't make head or tail of it,' Arthur agreed. 'And that's saying something, given how good we've got at working things out recently.'

'Some of it made sense though,' Billie said. 'What he said about there being other people like the Islanders, for instance . . . Other people who need help.'

'*There will be more*, those were his words.' Arthur jotted with his leaky old pen in his notepad. '*There will be more* . . .'

Harry kept looking out through the window. Directly below, a crowd was gathering around the steps and he made out the mayor, tottering down them with Auntie May, Brother Jacques, and the other Islanders. The crowd pushed forward but there were no brandished placards, no shaking fists, and no furious faces. Instead, the crowd's cries were joyful ones, and people were reaching out to shake the Islanders' hands. A very different crowd, Harry observed, and a bigger one too. The mayor marched off up the street with the Islanders, heading in the direction of Fisherman's Point.

*Their rightful home.*

Harry's heart throbbed and his pulses twitched. He could feel those little flickering sensations too, very gently travelling over his skin. *Just like before a trick.* He heard a clattering noise and saw that Billie and Arthur were dismantling the telephone, Billie pulling a long ribbon of paper from the machine's insides. On it seemed to be written some sort of complicated code. Harry watched his friends' faces, intent, curious, determined. At the sight of them, the last traces of scorpion venom fled. He smiled, turned back to the window, and watched the mayor and the Islanders reach the end of the street, turn a corner, and disappear from view.

He looked at his hand. The fingers were moving so fast they were almost a blur.

'You're right, Artie,' he said. *'There'll be more.'*

# Five Ways to Continue the Thrills!

Young Houdini:
The Magician's Fire

The Dangerous Discoveries
of Gully Potchard

Young Knights of the
Round Table

Dark Summer

The Mysterious Misadventure
of Clemency Wrigglesworth